FORBIDDEN:
THE BILLIONAIRE'S
VIRGIN PRINCESS

FORBIDDEN: THE BILLIONAIRE'S VIRGIN PRINCESS

BY

LUCY MONROE

MILLS & BOON®
Pure reading pleasure™

First published in Great Britain 2008
Large Print edition 2008
Harlequin Mills & Boon Limited,
Eton House, 18-24 Paradise Road,
Richmond, Surrey TW9 1SR

20183356

© Lucy Monroe 2008

ISBN: 978 0 263 20091 1

Set in Times Roman 16¾ on 20 pt.
16-1108-43562

Printed and bound in Great Britain
by CPI Antony Rowe, Chippenham, Wiltshire

For all the readers who wanted Hawk's story.
Thank you for writing me. And with special thanks to
Mills & Boon® for letting this, my twentieth story for
them, be part of their amazing 100 years
and still going legacy!

CHAPTER ONE

LINA MARWAN stood on the edge of the bridge, her eyes shut as she searched for her center.

A slight breeze caressed her sun warmed skin. It was a beautiful day to be alive. She released the railing and nothing stood between her and open air…a fifty-foot drop to the rushing waters of the river below.

Adrenaline coursed through her at the thought of what she was about to do. Her breaths came in short pants and sweat formed on her temples and palms. She curled her fingers into fists and then released them several times as she forced her lungs into a more relaxed rhythm.

Loud voices from behind her disturbed the peace she was trying to attain. Opening her eyes, she looked back over her shoulder and saw him.

Sebastian Hawk.

The last person she expected to see at this moment in her life. The last man she expected, or wanted, to see ever again. Before, or after, death. God wouldn't be so cruel as to put her and the deceitful bastard in the same part of heaven.

Well, there was nothing for it. He was here and it would only be a matter of seconds before he convinced the officials holding him off the bridge into letting him come for her.

She faced forward again, spread her arms like wings and let her body fall forward as the sound of Sebastian's roar echoed off the ravine's rocky walls.

Soaring through the air like a bird diving for its prey, memories from eight years before flooded Lina's mind in a reel-to-reel play of her time with Sebastian Hawk.

* * *

Headed toward the University Center, Lina rushed across the quad. She was late for the meeting, but it couldn't be helped. She'd had to ditch her bodyguard. Again. He was reading a book on Ancient Egypt on the ground floor of the library. He believed she was in a study group meeting in one of the rooms on the second floor. If the poor man knew how many hours he spent in the library while she was elsewhere, they would both be in a lot of trouble.

He was easy to fool. Too easy for her ego. In his mind her high grade point average attested unequivocally to many hours spent studying. She did study, just not nearly as much as he believed. However, like her father and far too many other men from her country, her guard did not believe a woman could get the grades she did without putting a huge effort into the task. All of the guards in her current security detail were similarly afflicted in their thinking.

When she had discovered the benefits to this

particular formerly annoying trait she had been grateful for her father's insistence on supplying her bodyguards from her home country for the first time.

Raised in America since she was six, she'd often chafed at the attitudes exhibited by her Marwanian guards. Then she had arrived at university and discovered how easy it was to gain temporary freedom on the pretext of studying. She grinned. Life might not be perfect, but it certainly was fun.

Her grin changed to a grimace as she ran into a rock wall dressed like a man.

She bounced backward, landing right on her bum in the grass. "Ooof."

"Are you all right?" Oh, wow. The rock wall had a voice that made her insides ping.

She looked up…and up…a couple of inches over six feet of *rippling* muscle, until their eyes met. His were gray. A dark, mysterious gunmetal gray. Though, right at that moment, their expression was perfectly readable. They were lit with concern. For her.

Nice.

Her smile returned and she stuck her hand out. "Fine. Thanks. Give me a lift?"

His lips quirked. "Certainly." He reached toward her and their hands connected.

Starbursts might have gone off, she wasn't sure. Because the momentum from his tug landed her body against his and her senses went supernova. Her dazzled brain registered that his mouth was still curved in that half-curve. She wondered what he'd look like with a full-blown smile. Devastating, probably. She probably wouldn't survive it.

"You sure you're okay?" he asked, looking really concerned now.

And darned if she didn't *really* like that. "Wonderful."

"You don't need help to remain standing?"

"No." Did she look like she needed help?

"Then, maybe you'd like to let go? Not that I mind the close contact." Warm amusement laced his words.

"I should…let go I mean." But her body made no effort to move backward.

He laughed. "My name is Sebastian Hawk."

Ulp. His laughter sent shivers through her as she found herself mesmerized by the absolutely gorgeous smile that accompanied it. Okay, so she'd survived a close encounter with his smile, but wasn't so sure about her mental faculties.

This man was very destructive to rational thought processes.

"And you are?"

Right. Very bad for normal brain activity.

"Oh, I'm Lina Marwan." She never used her complete name Lina bin Fahd al Marwan anymore.

"It's a pleasure to meet you, Lina," he said as he gently set her away from him.

She had to fight the urge to press forward and reconnect. Was this what it felt like to be attracted to a man? If it was, she could now be glad she'd spent her teen years at an all-girls school. Unlike her classmates, she'd never had the opportunity to spend time with boys her own age during school breaks. Her family kept too close of tabs on her for that.

In the year and a half since she came to university, she'd hugged a couple of boys, friends she met in her secret pursuits, but they'd never affected her like Sebastian Hawk. She'd always wanted to know what it was like to kiss a boy, but only in the abstract. Now she wanted to know the very concrete reality of kissing Sebastian Hawk.

The craving was so strong, her lips twitched. Sebastian's gray gaze was knowing—as if he could read the unfamiliar desire surging through her.

The tower clock chimed the quarter hour across the quad and Lina's body jolted with memory.

"Shoot. I'm late. I hope I haven't missed my chance to sign up for the kayaking trip." She still hadn't worked out completely how she was going to get away from her bodyguard and family for an entire weekend, but she was determined to go on this trip.

"You kayak?" Sebastian asked in a surprised tone.

"It's one of my favorite things. Not that I get to go as often as I like." She started walking briskly toward the University Center.

He kept pace with her. "When did you learn?"

"In high school." There were benefits to being the *female* offspring to a Middle Eastern king.

Sure, at first, when she'd been sent away from all that she knew, she'd felt abandoned. But as she'd grown older, she'd realized her parents' lack of interest in her daily life was to her benefit. They were very conservative and that attitude influenced their Americanized relatives they'd placed her with at the tender age of six.

However, she still had more freedom living with her relatives than she would ever have had at home. And she'd gotten her first taste of real freedom when she'd gone to boarding school in seventh grade. The exclusive, all-girls prep school was far from the typical American middle and high schools, but she'd been allowed to do things there she would never have been able to do when living with family. Things like kayaking.

"I see. I thought the kayaking trip was a three-day get-away."

"It is. Are you going?" she asked, unable to stifle the hope in her gaze as her eyes remained locked with those of the tall, dark-haired hunk.

She felt the same adrenaline rush she got when competing in a race. Man, this being attracted to a guy thing was nothing like she'd expected it to be. It was almost scarily consuming. As exciting as taking a kayak out on white water. Maybe even more so.

Hawk had to bite down on an ugly four-letter word.

The diminutive princess was just full of surprises. The first had been when he'd seen his newest charge hurrying across the quad when she was supposed to be safely ensconced in the library studying with a small group of female friends. The plan had been for him to confer with her bodyguard and then arrange to "bump into" the princess on her way out of the library later.

It was a good thing he'd seen her, or he would have been just as ignorant of her true whereabouts as her hapless guard. The man needed to take a course in security from Hawk Investigations.

"I don't kayak," he said to her, "but I'd like to learn." Which was a total lie. He had no desire to learn, but he had experienced canoeing. Even if it wasn't his favorite thing, it was close enough to the other that he was confident he would make a good showing of himself on the water.

A man did what he had to for his job. And Hawk's current assignment was sticking close to Princess Lina bin Fahd al Marwan.

Her smile was dazzling. "If we hurry, maybe we'll both still get a chance to sign up for the trip."

Options clicked through Hawk's mind. One, he could prevent her from making the meeting at all. Two, he could scuttle any chances she had of going on the trip with a single phone call. *Or* he could follow his instincts and go on the trip with her.

Her obvious attraction to him would make it easy to arrange for her to miss the meeting, but *this woman* would probably find a way to sign up for the trip regardless. Lina Marwan, as she called herself, was nothing like the shy, quiet, studious, nineteen-year-old he had been led to expect.

Did anyone in the princess's life know who she really was and how she amused herself?

The answer was no doubt in the negative, which was why he also did not want to scuttle the trip entirely.

He'd been hired as extra security during a time of increased risk for the Royal Family of Marwan. However, if his interaction had the benefit of allowing him to help her security detail enhance her overall safety—so much the better. He had to identify the ways she circumvented it in order to prevent her from doing so in the future.

Letting her make the trip while he accompanied her to ensure her safety, would give him the opportunity to see what measures she took to avoid her security detail.

He made all these determinations in the space of seconds.

"Lead the way," he said with a smile.

She nodded, but instead of increasing her pace, she stopped, her dark brown gaze fixed on his lips.

"Lina…"

"Uh, yeah, right…go." She made a visible effort to look away. Flipping her long black ponytail over her shoulder, she started jogging toward the University Center. "The meeting was supposed to be upstairs."

His long strides matched her speed with little effort, but his body heated in reaction to the enticing bounce of her feminine curves. The attraction was definitely mutual, which should make his job that much easier. He wouldn't have to pretend an interest to stay close to her. Though his original intention had been to strike up a friendship, being just slightly more than friends would be an even better "in" to the princess's life.

However, he would only take it so far. He didn't do long-term and for so many reasons, Lina was not a candidate for a short-term affair. Not only was she the daughter of a client and herself his assignment, but she was a princess from a part of the world that placed a lot of importance on a woman's virginity. It wouldn't be fair to the princess to take their association beyond friendship and mild flirting.

Although he had a sense of honor that would not allow him to use the innocent, he was *not* above using her attraction to him.

Lina stopped in front of an athletic-looking blond man who had been coming down the steps in front of the U.C. "Hey, Bob. Did we miss the meeting?"

"Yeah, but no biggie. All we did was pass out info sheets and take names."

"Can we still sign up?" she asked enthusiastically.

The jock put his hand on Lina's shoulder and squeezed, his smile practiced and more than a little flirtatious. "Anything for you, sweetie."

Another curse fought for release from Hawk's mouth. Did she have a boyfriend her family didn't know about, too?

"Great." The diminutive princess bounced on the balls of her feet. "Sebastian's a new kayaker. I'd like him assigned with me…" She turned to look at Hawk. "I mean if you don't have an issue with a woman teaching you."

"No, I'd like that."

"Hey, Wayne could train the newbie and then you could be *my* partner," Bob suggested.

"*The newbie* would prefer to partner his new friend." It was the *only* way the princess was getting out on the water. A bodyguard could hardly do his job from the shore or another boat.

"Oh, I'm sorry. We didn't mean to talk about you like you weren't there." Lina's doelike eyes shone with genuine repentance. "I hate it when people do that to me."

He supposed, considering the strongly conservative and male centered family she came from, she'd had a lot of experience with it, too. "No problem." But the look he gave Bob told the other man not to mess with him.

From the expression on the college boy's face, he got the message, but didn't look happy about it. Again Hawk wondered if the relationship between Bob and Lina was closer than merely friends with a mutual interest in kayaking.

"Look, I'll sign you both up, but I'll need your contact details," Bob said to Hawk. "I've got Lina's. In fact, I already signed you up, babe. I was going to bring you the info sheet in World Politics."

Lina smiled at Bob, her eyes lit with gratitude and excitement. "You're the best. Thanks."

Bob slipped his backpack off his shoulder and

dug out a notebook. "Here, just put your stuff in here." He didn't let go of the notebook when Hawk reached for it, though. "You are a student here, right? This trip is only open to students at the university."

Lina frowned, but her expression cleared when Sebastian said, "I'm in the MBA program across the street."

"Oh. Okay then." Bob let go of the notebook.

Hawk took it and flipped through the pages until he came to a list of names under a hand-written title, "Kayaking Trip." He pulled his pen out of his pocket and took pictures of the list of names under the guise of clicking the pen open. He added his name and cover contact information to the bottom of the list.

He would have someone at Hawk Investigations run a report on the names on the list to make sure none of them represented a threat to Lina's safety.

He wondered how she planned to dupe her bodyguard for an entire weekend, but he had no doubt, whatever her plan was, she would succeed. A princess who had managed to become an expert kayaker *while* going to the exclusive boarding school she had attended without her family's knowledge was adept at getting around their strictures for her life.

Bob looked at his watch and then at Lina. "We've got almost an hour before class. Do you want to get coffee with me at the Starbucks on State Street?"

She bit her bottom lip and looked sideways at Hawk, then nodded. "Can we get our coffee at the cafeteria, though? I need to pick something up at the library before class."

Hawk almost laughed out loud. She had to pick something up all right...her bodyguard. "You don't mind if I tag along, do you?" he asked. "I could use a cup of coffee myself."

Lina's mouth curved into another blinding smile. "No, of course not. You'll have to let me buy, though. It's the least I can do after running into you in the quad."

"You're the one that ended up on the floor. I think I should buy."

Bob shook his head. "Whoever wants to buy, let's go. I need my fix of caffeine."

"Were you up studying late again last night?" Lina asked him.

"You could call it that."

She smacked his arm lightly. "You are so bad. Who was it this time? The sexy sorority girl with a boyfriend at a different school or the gymnast?"

"I'm not seeing the gymnast anymore. Her coach told her one more late night and lack of focus the next day and she was off the team."

So, Bob was a player. And Lina knew it. The question was, did he plan on adding Lina to his list of conquests? Not on Hawk's watch, he wouldn't. Her family had hired his agency to see to her safety and he would do so. On every front. What she and the jock-boy did when Hawk finished with the case was not his problem.

He studiously ignored the tightening in his gut that occurred at that particular thought.

The student cafeteria coffee wasn't bad. They even had an espresso machine. Not that Hawk drank specialty coffees, but both Lina and Bob did and from the hum of pleasure Lina emitted as she took her first sip, Hawk assumed it was good. He'd won the argument about him paying, but then he had expected to.

He wasn't in the habit of losing—at anything.

"Are you going to the environmental demonstration tonight?" Bob asked Lina as he leaned back in his chair, his gaze following a curvy coed cross the dining room.

"I'm not sure, but I'll try to be there."

"There's a rumor the Young Republicans are going to show up to heckle us."

"Well, if they do, they'll be heckling half their membership. Environmentalism isn't the partisan issue big politicians say it is. There are conservationists on both sides."

"If you say so."

"You know I do."

"Are you a political science student?" Hawk asked Lina, already knowing the answer, but wanting to get *her* to tell him more about herself. How much honesty was she willing to give?

"We both are," Bob answered for her. "Lina's a fence-sitter, though. She won't identify with either of our major parties."

Lina simply shrugged, but didn't mention what Hawk assumed was her real reason for not identifying with either party. She was a citizen of Marwan, not the United States.

"I'm not a Young Republican and it kills my dad." Bob's satisfied smirk said a lot about why *he* leaned to the left politically.

Lina sighed and shook her head. "I swear you go to the rallies simply out of reactionary rebellion."

"Didn't you tell me once that you decided to study politics because your dad told you not to?" Bob asked pointedly.

The princess nodded, not looking the least bit phased. "It was a little more complicated than that, but his negative reaction to my interest in the subject did spur me on. However, how I react to what I've learned in my studies is the result of personal convictions. I hold beliefs different from my family, but not because I want to get a rise out of my dad. I doubt he'd even deign to notice, but my family's political beliefs have had a strong and sometimes negative impact on my life."

"In what way?" Bob asked.

Lina merely shook her head and changed the subject. Apparently Bob was not a close enough friend to be aware of Lina's position as daughter to a desert king.

CHAPTER TWO

OVER THE NEXT WEEK, Hawk learned that, though Lina could be described as nothing less than *involved*, she had no friends that knew the truth about her. In fact, while she had many people she spent time with, she had none Hawk would classify as close friends period. At least the report about her he had received had been correct in that regard. Even if it had been wrong about so much else.

And *nothing* in the report had prepared him for the growing attraction between them. He had thought it would be something he could use to stay close to her, but discovered quickly that it was far more a detriment than a benefit in regard to doing his job.

How could he protect her when he was distracted by how her ebony hair shone in the sunlight? His fascination with her waist-length hair had been born the first time he saw her wear it down. It looked and felt like silk. And how did he know how it felt?

He couldn't stop himself from touching it. And Lina didn't seem to mind. While she shied away from a lot of physical touch from others, keeping hugs short and one-armed with even her female acquaintances, she leaned into Hawk's touch. Not that he had touched her… that way. But he wanted to. Badly. His fingers actually ached to brush against the luscious curves hidden under her clothing.

It wasn't that she wore anything overtly sexy, but it was the way she moved, with an innate sensuality he was certain she had no idea she possessed.

Like right now, she was sitting across from him at the Starbucks her friend Bob had first mentioned. The way she held her head in attention while Hawk spoke highlighted the delicate curve of her neck and drew his gaze down to breasts that were molded lovingly by the cotton of her T-shirt. He was pretty sure she wasn't wearing a bra. Or the one she had on was so thin she might as well not be wearing it, because for the last several minutes her nipples had been hard. His mouth was watering for a taste of the sweet flesh.

"Sebastian?" she asked in a soft…almost uncertain voice.

His gaze shot from her breasts to her face and he felt himself going red. When was the last time that happened? He was a twenty-seven-year-old millionaire in his own right. He'd left blushing boyhood behind too long ago to remember it, if indeed it had ever been a phase for him. "Yes?"

"I…uh…I wondered if you wanted…um…"

"Yes?"

She was silent for several seconds, chewing on her bottom lip, looking too damn delectable.

Then she said all in a rush, "Maybe we could go for a walk down State Street."

"Sure. If you've got the time." Once again, her regular bodyguard believed that she was studying. This time, at home.

When Hawk had learned Lina knew how to bypass the security and leave the apartment she shared with a chaperone next to the one that housed her security detail, he'd been ready to strangle somebody. Her bodyguards were at the top of Hawk's list. How many times had the princess left her home unprotected? Hawk had not revealed the security breach to the family retainers, though.

He was operating under the assumption that the threat to her family could be from within and he wasn't taking any risks. He would give a full report with detailed suggestions for improving security for the princess when this situation was over. He had another operative from his staff at Hawk Investigations watching Lina's building when he slept. And she was supposed to be sleeping. With the feisty princess one could never be sure.

Normally he would have the entire case assigned to his operatives, but Hawk had made his investigative agency an international contender and multimillion dollar company by knowing when it was prudent to take a personal interest in a client's needs. He'd certainly made the right call this time.

Lina moved close to him as they walked along the tree-lined street near the capitol building and, of its own volition, his arm snaked around her petite waist.

It was only natural considering his role, but it felt *too* good. Not only was she a client (even if she didn't know he was her paid protector), but Hawk didn't do affectionate gestures and warm fuzzy feelings. His liaisons with women were just that. Commitment free, exchanges of pleasure without any false protestations of emotion. He didn't even have female friends. He had no interest in getting serious with a woman. In any guise. Ever.

Every woman he had known had been devious in her own way. The woman who had given him birth had pretended maternal interest until the day she found a more lucrative benefactor than his father. She'd dumped them both and had contacted Hawk exactly twice in the intervening years. Both times she had wanted to use him. He'd let her the first time, but known enough to send her packing the second.

His grandmother was just as mercenary, though she'd stayed with Hawk's grandfather. He didn't know if the men in his family sucked at picking out women to share their lives with, or were simply unlucky. Either way, he'd managed to follow family tradition twice before establishing a firm rule about the type of relationship he was willing to have with the feminine sex.

Which was none at all. Not with the women related to him and not with the women who occasionally shared his bed.

While the things he felt around Lina were more intense and harder to control, he *had* to control them. Because she was no different than the other women in his life he should have been able to trust.

She lied to her security detail and family on a regular basis. Would she be any more trustworthy in a relationship?

He didn't think so. After all, she hadn't yet told him the true nature of her life. They might not be in a relationship and she wasn't even a candidate for a brief liaison. But she didn't know that. As far as she knew, their flirtatious friendship could go anywhere. Yet she still maintained the deception about her life.

And that life—her existence as a princess—was one reason the depth of his desire for her was so completely unacceptable. Even if she wasn't his assignment, an affair would carry too many complications with it.

Not only was there the whole virginity thing, but Lina herself was not the type of woman to be content with a little, or even a lot, of between the sheets pleasure. She was more the type to believe in everlasting love and the whole fantasy that went along with it.

He might not trust her. He may be more cynical than other men still naïve to the ways of women, but Hawk wasn't about to be the cause of Lina's shattered fantasies. That would happen soon enough. Life would see to it.

Not even a princess was immune.

On top of all of that, Hawk had worked too hard to build his company into an international power player in the industry. He wasn't risking its reputation for a woman. No matter how enticing she was.

Flashing faster than instantaneous replay, scene after scene of her time with Sebastian rolled across the movie screen in Lina's mind.

Sebastian had offered to drive her to the kayaking excursion in his car. A Dodge Viper, the same gunmetal gray of his eyes, the powerful sports car didn't have room for anyone else. So they would spend the ninety-minute drive to the campground alone. She found her attention occupied by his profile and the way his powerful thighs bulged in his jeans, rather than the admittedly gorgeous scenery out the window.

She'd spent endless hours thinking about this man, trying to decide if he was as interested in her as she was in him.

She had no experience and no one she felt comfortable going to for advice. That left her with her own opinion based on…well nothing. Okay, there'd been the gossip from other girls in high school, but none of it seemed to apply. Sebastian wasn't pushing for sex or copping a feel every time they were in a remotely private place.

She thought it was probably because he was older, a graduate student who already had some experience in the business world.

She was pretty sure he desired her, though. The way he looked at her at times made her brain melt. And other bits as well.

She'd tried reading women's magazines, but they all touted open communication in a relationship. Did that mean she was supposed to just *ask* him?

She would rather pick up on nonverbal clues. And she was convinced there were some.

Sometimes, his eyes would gleam with something that responded to the ache deep in her womb whenever he was around. But he had never acted on it and they had been seeing each other for three weeks now. They hadn't had any dates per se, but he'd been around pretty much constantly since she'd run into him in the quad.

Since he did not seem like a big joiner, the fact that he was at meetings she'd never before seen him at or rallies she was pretty sure he had no personal interest in, she had to assume *she* was the reason he showed up. Which meant he wanted her, right?

It amazed her, really. That a man like Sebastian would be interested in Lina Marwan was pretty incredible. She was accustomed to people being drawn by her royal status, but like the rest of the students at the university, he had no way of knowing she was a princess. But he liked her…maybe…

He was everything she had dreamed of finding in a boyfriend, not that he was actually her boyfriend.

She sighed. Sebastian gave her a questioning look. She smiled a little and shrugged. Thankfully he didn't ask her what she was thinking. She might just blurt it out and embarrass herself unbearably.

He was so gorgeous; he was assertive without being domineering. He listened to her, maybe even better than her brother. He was smart and driven—his going for an MBA showed that. And he was intense in this really, super sexy way. Was it any surprise she was falling for Sebastian Hawk in a big way?

The problem was that sometimes she was convinced that all he wanted was friendship.

She was so bad at this whole male-female thing. Her lack of practical experience was becoming a real nuisance. If she had been like the other girls who attended the female-only academy she had, she would have at least had a chance when not in school to meet people of the opposite gender. To learn to *flirt* for goodness sake. Though she had to admit that even if she had the opportunity, the male dominant nature of her family had made her wary around men and she probably would have shied away from any sort of interaction.

That caution combined with the reality that in order to date it would have meant further deceptions, or the indignity of being subjected to not only a bodyguard, but a chaperone as well, had also kept her from pursuing or responding to the pursuit of any guys since she'd arrived at university. Until Sebastian.

Of course, it helped that he was willing to

spend time with her doing the things she already arranged for involvement in.

Only…for this man, she would do whatever it took to see him personally. She just wished she knew *what* to do with him.

Not that lack of experience had ever stopped her from trying something that she wanted to. She was not the demure, ornamental—aka useless—piece of feminity her father believed her to be.

Sebastian was so different from the men in her family. He never dismissed her thoughts as un-important simply because she wasn't heir to a throne or provincial position. He wasn't sur-prised by her intelligence and he didn't seem to think her political science major was a waste of her time. Not that he knew why she had chosen that major, but he acted like he believed she could, and most likely *would*, do something valuable with her education.

That was her hope.

She'd spent her childhood separated from her

home, only to see her parents and siblings one week out of the year when she flew to Marwan and stayed in the royal palace with them. She did not remember her parents ever touching her with affection, and knew for a fact her father had never once given her any recognition as anything but his inferior female offspring.

She refused to spend her adult life feeling and *being* insignificant. She wanted to make a difference in the world and not merely as the attractive, well mannered appendage on some man's arm.

"You're pretty quiet over there," Sebastian said.

"I was thinking how different you are from the men in my family."

"Yes?"

"Yes."

"In what way?"

"You don't discount me simply because I'm female."

"Who does that?"

"My father. To some extent my uncle. Others."

"Your brother?"

She didn't remember mentioning her brother, but she must have done so. She gave one of the rare smiles that occurred when she thought of her family. "My brother is different. He has been raised to be just like my father, but he's not. You can't tell on the surface, but he does special things to let me know."

"Like what?" Sebastian's obviously genuine interest encouraged her to be more open with the truth than she would have normally.

"He spends time with me."

"Don't your parents?"

"My mother does...sort of." Though the sessions spent training Lina for her station could hardly be classified as mother-daughter bonding time.

"Not your father?" Sebastian didn't sound surprised or disapproving, simply curious.

"No. He's far too busy to spend quality time with a mere daughter." Though, according to her sister, their father made limited time available to his daughter still living in Marwan.

"That bothers you?"

"Wouldn't it you?"

He looked a little startled and then shrugged. "I suppose. But in my case it was my mother that couldn't be bothered to see me. My dad is and has always been pretty busy with his business interests, too, though."

"And that doesn't upset you?"

"Why should it? I'm busy with my own life."

"So, you don't think a family should spend time together?"

"You mean the dream of dinners together and family camping trips every summer?"

"Something like that."

"If you're born into a family like that, I'm sure it's nice. But if you aren't, you have to accept your circumstances and move forward."

"Or change them."

Again, he looked surprised by her comment. "How would you do that?"

"Me, personally? I plan to marry someone who believes family is as important as I do or I won't marry at all. I will spend time getting to know my children, if I have any. No son *or* daughter of mine will grow up feeling expendable."

"You think you are expendable to your parents?"

"I know I am."

"Why do you say that?"

"I came to the U.S. at the age of six because my mother's older sister had been unable to conceive and it was decided that she would be given the honor of raising me. I only see my parents once a year, for a week." She never ever gave details of her life to people, but Sebastian was different. She trusted him.

"And your brother?"

She smiled again, warmth filling her at thoughts of her brother. "When I'm staying with my parents, he makes sure we eat at least one meal together each day. And we talk. He asks about my life and *listens* to my answers. He praises me for my grades and other things. He's the only person in my family who knows that I was on the kayaking team at school. He also makes sure he comes to visit me every time he is in America. My father flies to Washington, D.C., at least twice a year, but he's never once made the additional effort to come see me as well. Even when he and my brother are traveling together and Hasim makes arrangements to do so."

"I'm sure he's confident that you are well taken care of by your aunt and uncle."

"I am. I don't want to denigrate them in any way to you. My aunt is sweet, if a bit reserved, and my uncle is much more open to new ideas than my father, having been raised himself in Canada. He was a third son. Though sometimes family attitudes still show, I was allowed to attend university only at his insistence. If it had been up to my parents, I would have gone to a finishing school in Europe." Even after her father had agreed to her university education, Lina had taken the added precaution of pursuing United States citizenship as soon as she turned eighteen.

It had taken her two years and had been the

reason she'd learned to ditch her bodyguard as well as how to get out of her home undetected. She had two sets of papers. Her Marwanian papers, which she used traveling under the aegis of her country's ruling family. She also had legitimate U.S. passport and citizenship papers, which her family knew nothing about.

As a Marwanian citizen, her father had had final say over anything and everything in her life, no matter what her age. That was not true for all Marwanian women, but as a member of the ruling family, she could not legally act without her father's permission. However, as an adult U.S. Citizen, her freedoms were numerous including the right to refuse to return to Marwan if it became necessary.

"But your relationship with your parents makes you unhappy?"

"My *lack* of a relationship. Like I said, if I have children, I want a different life for them."

"I am sure you will succeed at whatever you set your mind to."

She gave him a glowing smile. She was definitely falling in love with this man. "Thank you."

When they arrived at the cabins the kayaking group was staying in, Hawk noticed only one other car there. It turned out to be Bob's. He and three more members of the group were still unloading. Hawk made sure that he was in one of the bedrooms of the cabin Lina was staying in. He noticed that Bob did, too. In fact, they were sharing the room. Which worked for Hawk. He was a fan of efficiency and this would allow him to keep an eye on both the princess and her wannabe hook-up.

Lina was sharing her room with one of the other coeds. A blonde who looked like a pinup and talked like G.I. Jane. Lina told Hawk when they were reconnoitering the lake (well he was surveying their environment, Lina was just walking) that the blonde was former military and had just started university this semester.

Hawk had known *that* from his agency's reports. What he hadn't known was that Lina's admiration for the other woman's independence and lifestyle bordered on hero-worship.

"She's been to seedy bars in more countries of the world than I've even visited."

"And you see this as a good thing?" Hawk asked.

Lina's laugh was joyous and too damned appealing to his libido. "Yes. My life has been so sheltered. A weekend like this is as about as adventurous as I've ever gotten."

"But you want more adventure?" Hawk asked with a sinking feeling. If her family didn't beef up Lina's security, she would get that adventure. She was too resourceful not to.

"Yes. I want to travel. I want to do things... help people. See the world, but not as a member of...um...the privileged classes. As someone trying to make a difference."

"You make it sound like you want to join the Peace Corps."

"That's one of my dreams, but I doubt I'll ever realize it."

Hawk had to take a deep breath or choke on his surprise. A princess in the Peace Corps? He didn't think so. "If you can't have a dream, find a practical replacement." Like donating money to worthy causes. That was something a princess could do without causing a political incident.

Lina stopped walking and stared out over the lake, her expression thoughtful. Hawk stopped, too…but he watched his princess. Her golden skin glowing in the sunlight, her perfect features shone with a beauty that took his breath away. Of its own volition, his hand reached out and brushed her hair away from her face.

She shifted slightly so their eyes met, her velvet-brown irises drawing him in, her smile tempting him to taste her lips. Her head tilted; his dipped until their lips barely brushed. Electricity jolted through him at the contact, freezing time around them. Neither moved.

They did not deepen the kiss, but nor did they move apart. Both stood in a paralysis of feeling he knew he had never experienced and suspected she had not, either.

They were only linked physically in two places—his lips barely touching hers and his hand still against her cheek—but he felt the connection in a place deep inside that he had not even known existed.

"Hey, you two." Bob's voice brought Hawk abruptly to his senses.

Yanking his hand away from her cheek, Hawk stepped away from Lina.

What the hell was he doing? He hadn't even heard Bob's approach. This was totally out of line. He would fire an operative for being so sloppy. If Bob had been a threat, Lina could be dead right now. Cold chills chased along his skin.

He was here to protect Lina, not make love to her. Or moon over her like some lovesick calf. He was not the mooning type.

Maybe he needed a vacation. One filled with discreet liaisons that would rid his mind of his…*the* princess's image.

One thing he knew with certainty. The idealistic pocket-size Venus was turning out to be a weakness he could not afford, "Hi, Bob." Lina's voice was softer than normal and her eyes were unfocused.

Hawk had to suppress a groan. This *thing* was getting totally out of hand. *It already was*, a taunting voice whispered inside his head. Bob gave them both a knowing look. "This is supposed to be a sports trip, not a romantic getaway."

Sebastian glared at Bob. As if jock-boy wouldn't take advantage if he got the chance. And he'd have a hell of a lot less scruples about it than Sebastian did.

Lina looked away, her cheeks going an adorable pink.

"Was there something you wanted, Bob?" Hawk asked. Trying to forget that the word adorable was not usually part of his vocabulary and that he had applied it to a client.

"Just thought I'd check the lake out. We'll start out on the smooth water tomorrow morning. Assess everyone's skill level, then move to the river after lunch tomorrow." He gave Hawk a significant look. "That is provided we're all ready to move to the river."

Hawk was about to assure the other man that *he* would be ready when Lina spoke up. "If Sebastian isn't comfortable enough for moving water, I'll stay on the lake with him in the afternoon."

And just like that, Hawk's plans for proving his proficiency changed. "If you're sure you won't mind," he said.

Bob frowned. "That's hardly fair to you, babe. I'm sure one of the other experienced kayakers would be willing to stay with him."

Hawk noticed Bob didn't volunteer.

Lina's features set in what was becoming a familiar look of stubbornness. "Don't be silly.

I invited Sebastian to come on the trip. I promised him I would teach him and I will."

Which was exactly what she did. Hawk's previous experience canoeing made learning the balance and movement of the kayak easier, but Lina was also a good teacher and could take most of the credit for his proficiency by afternoon. He was careful to dump into the water a couple of times though to lend credence to his request to stay on the lake for the rest of the day.

They all ate lunch together in the biggest cabin. Lina was animated and grinning most of the time, praising him for his efforts and complimenting the others on their techniques. She and her roommate got into a discussion of what their most challenging kayaking course had been. And that's when he learned that Lina had come very near to drowning once, sending a sick feeling through him.

Her senior year of high school, while on a very difficult race course, another kayaker had dumped. She'd bumped her head and hadn't come up. Lina dove into the white water to save her. Both girls had come close to drowning, but Lina had managed to get them to shore.

Hawk experienced an unexpected, unfamiliar, and not to mention totally irrational fear as Lina recounted her story. That fear did not dissipate when Lina looked on with wide-eyed wonder and no small amount of interest when her G.I. Jane roommate recounted shooting the rapids on the Yangtze River. Damn…if Lina's family didn't do something soon, she was going to get herself killed in her search for adventure.

She needed a husband to watch over her.

Heaven knew her father, uncle and their hired security weren't doing a good enough job. Unreasoning black anger washed over Hawk at the thought of a protective male in Lina's life that was not him. He dismissed the image of Lina in some faceless man's arms with a vicious precision he refused to analyze.

CHAPTER THREE

HE AND Lina finished on the lake before the others returned from the river and she suggested going swimming.

"Haven't you spent enough time in the water?" Hawk asked, having to admit privately that he had enjoyed his time on the water more than he ever had in the past.

Lina shrugged, smiling. "I love water. Maybe I should have been born a dolphin."

"Oh, no. I think you make a perfect woman." Hawk had to stifle a growl. He should not have said that. Things were getting out of hand with his princess. But he couldn't deny the warmth that shot through him as her smile increased wattage. "Thank you," she said happily without a hint of a woman's usual coyness at such a compliment.

They pulled the kayaks up onto the shore, took off their slim life vests and jumped back into the water. At least he did, but when he turned to see where Lina was, she was on the beach still, peeling off the Neoprene suit she'd been wearing to kayak in. The very brief bikini she wore underneath made the air stall in Hawk's chest.

Damn. She had a luscious figure. Her breasts were a little oversized, her waist tiny above the flare of her hips, her legs toned and smooth. And that damned scrap of cloth that passed for bikini bottoms showed way more skin than it covered and clung to the perfect curve of her backside. She kicked the wet suit aside and walked back into the water.

She stopped a few feet from him, her head cocked to one side, her doe-brown gaze questioning. "Something wrong?"

"Uh—" He had to clear his throat. "No. Nothing. You sure you don't want to wear your

Neoprene to swim in? It's warm for spring, but not exactly hot out here."

"I'm fine." But she shuddered with a full body shiver, belying her words. She smiled self-deprecatingly. "Well, I'll warm up swimming, anyway."

Her body was covered in goose bumps, but it was the hard nubs of her nipples behind her scant bikini top that drew his gaze.

And held it.

He watched in inescapable fascination as the wet lycra of her swimsuit did nothing to hide how the already hardened pebbles tightened into fine points.

"Sebastian…" The husky desire mixed with confusion in her voice was a potent aphrodisiac.

She wanted him and didn't know what to do with that need. What man would not be drawn by that combination of innocence and feminine awakening?

She did not move, her body frozen there, half in the water. Her breathing increased to pants, further revealing arousal so unfamiliar to her.

Her small hands fisted at her sides, her knuckles turning white.

Had any woman exhibited such intense desire for him?

Perhaps it was the result of Lina's innocence. Hawk hadn't had a virgin since high school. He had a strict policy of keeping his liaisons limited to experienced women who weren't looking for a relationship much less a lifelong commitment.

So, what the hell was he doing looking at Lina like a wolf did his prey?

He forced his gaze to lift to hers. And it was worse. The evidence of her interest in him shone brightly in her doe-brown eyes. Damn it.

Unblinking, her gaze fixed to his, she bit her bottom lip and damn if he didn't want to replace her teeth with his.

If he didn't do something soon, he was going to end up giving her her first time right here in the lake. His entire body vibrated with the need to go to her.

It took every ounce of his formidable self-control to turn and dive into the cold water. When he came up fifteen yards from the shore, she was only a few feet behind him.

Treading water, she grinned. "You aren't supposed to dunk yourself, don't you know that?"

"Oh, really?"

"Yes, really." Without further warning, she launched herself toward him.

Her hands pushed against his head and he let himself go under as his training took over and he used her momentum to get her into a hold she had no hope of getting out of. He brought them both up, breaking above the water to the trill of her laughter.

Her smile was unrepentant. "Now, that's how you're supposed to get dunked."

"You sure about that?"

"Of course. It's in the rules."

"The rules?"

"You know, the playing in the water rules?" she asked, her eyes lit with a mischievous spark.

"I don't know those rules."

"Why is that I wonder?"

"Maybe because I don't play."

"Everybody plays."

"Not me."

"Then I suppose I'll have to teach you how."

His mind immediately latched onto several images of things he would like to teach her. And not a single one of them was anywhere as innocent as playing in the water.

"You're doing it again."

"Doing what?" he asked, genuinely confused.

"Looking at me like you want to eat me."

He stared at her, for once speechless.

She laughed as she kicked out of his now lax hold. When she was several feet closer to the shore, she stopped and faced him, her chin just above the waterline. "What does that mean? The look."

"I…" He didn't know what to say to diffuse the situation. Sure as certain not the truth.

She took another couple of steps backward so the water wasn't so deep around her. Her head cocked to one side and she looked at him like a chemistry lab experiment that wasn't going the way she expected. She started chewing on that way-too-kissable, full lower lip of hers again.

Then she nodded as if making some kind of internal decision. "Look, I'm not very experienced at this sexual attraction thing. Okay?"

He nodded because it seemed like she wanted a response.

"Good. Some guys...especially ones a few years older than me, would be put off by that."

"Uh..."

"Don't worry about it. I'm glad you're not, but the problem is, I don't know what stuff means. Like that look you were giving me..." Her voice trailed off and she looked away, clearly uncomfortable with the direction of their conversation.

For which he felt profound gratitude. "Do you really want to talk about this?"

"Um...no...I just—"

"You're doing fine."

"I am?"

"Yes." That, at least, was safe to say.

"Oh, good then…I…"

He took advantage of her preoccupation and dove for her, figuring that her idea of water play had to be better than talking about the overwhelming attraction between them that should be *anything but* on his side. She expelled her air in a shocked gasp as she fell backward under his weight.

Without thought, he sealed his lips over hers, breathing his air into her lungs as they went under the water together.

He twisted his body and brought them both up again, breaking the connection of their mouths as water ran in rivulets down their faces.

She shook her head, laughing. "That was wild."

He tried to dunk her again, but this time she was ready for him and slipped out of his grasp. They played like that until she was gasping, "Uncle, uncle…I give, I give."

"I'm not your uncle, but I'm glad to hear you recognize my superior water playing skills."

"Funny, funny." She sighed and relaxed, linking her hands behind his neck. Then, she wrapped her legs around his waist. "That's better. You wore me out."

"Poor you," he choked out, trying to maintain some semblance of distance with her attached to him like a limpet.

Was he the one who had thought playing in the water was safer than talking? After fifteen minutes of her hands gliding over his body as she attempted to pull him under the water, he was hard as a rock and twice as hungry for her taste. And now, apparently she considered him her resting place. The position of her legs around his waist was way too tempting for the precarious control he had over his libido.

"It might just have a little to do with the fact that you are almost a foot taller than me."

"What?" he asked, having totally lost the train of their conversation. Hell, he was in a different depot entirely.

"The reason you won our water fight. You're

bigger than me…it gives you an unfair advantage in the deeper water."

"You should have kept us in the shallow water then. It's all about strategy."

"I'll remember that." Her gaze flicked to his lips…and stayed there. Her small pink tongue darted out to lick her own lips as they parted in unconscious but unmistakable invitation.

That one small move was the final nail in the coffin of Hawk's control and he did what he'd been wanting to do since they got in the water. He leaned down and took her bottom lip between his teeth. He sucked on it gently as she made a soft, surprised sound.

That sound went through him like an electric shock and his arms locked around her, pulling her body fully against his. She fit like she'd been created to be just there.

Her eyes opened, their chocolate depths glazed with passion. She was so beautiful…so perfect in her arousal.

He gave into the silent plea in her gaze and

kissed her, taking her mouth fully with lips, teeth and tongue. She whimpered, her body writhing in unconscious abandon against him. He memorized her body with his fingertips, touching every centimeter of skin he could reach.

She broke her mouth from his, wildly turning her head side to side. "Sebastian!"

"It's okay…let me touch you. You were made for my touch." He paid little attention to what he was saying, his words a natural outpouring from his desire.

However, there remained a small flicker of awareness in the back of his mind. That marginal ability for rational thought was surprised and maybe even a little worried at the possessiveness of his own words.

"Yes." She pressed into his hands, her own kneading his neck like she didn't know what to do with them.

He had just enough presence of mind not to encourage her to return the caresses.

He cupped the indent of her waist, marveling at the perfection of the curve. Even with the conservative protection of her family, it was unbelievable to him that she remained so untouched. Her natural sensuality and beauty were an irresistible aphrodisiac.

She kissed him back with unfettered passion while her body trembled with a need he was only too greedy to fulfill. However, he would not make love to her for the first time in the middle of a lake. There were many ways to satisfy the conflagration burning between them that did not require him buried in her virginal body. And if it took the last shred of his sanity, he would do those things rather than claim her body irrevocably as his.

He moved them a little closer to shore until the water lapped against his chest and then he peeled her arms from around his neck. She whimpered in protest.

"It is all right, little beauty. Trust me. I will give you what you are craving."

"Please, Sebastian." She looked at him with needy innocence.

She had no clue what she was asking for, or what he could give her. But he would show her…if nothing else, he would hold the distinction of being her first sexual teacher. He could not have more…they could not have more, but this he would have.

He flipped her around so her back was to his front and he leaned down so his mouth was against the shell of her ear. "I am going to make you feel so good, princess."

"P-princess?" she gasped out.

He stiffened in shock at his slip, but then decided to go with it. The term princess was used by a lot of American men as an endearment. He reasoned that she was Americanized enough to know that. "You are my princess."

Damn, there went that possessiveness again. He decided to go with it too. For now.

Her head fell back onto his shoulder. "Yes, your princess."

"Put your arms around my neck again."

She nodded, but he had to help her get her hands locked in place. She was that out of it… because of him. He made no attempt to stifle the sense of pride that she gave him.

He gently bit her earlobe while one hand caressed her stomach below the water. "Perfect."

She undulated against him, her body brushing his steel hard shaft. Pleasure shuddered through him despite the layers between them. He had never reacted so strongly to such a limited touch, but he had no such plans to restrict his own contact.

He undid the lower strap on her bikini top with his unoccupied hand, running his fingertips along where the strap had touched her. She shivered and made an inarticulate sound.

"Like that?" he asked in a whisper right against her ear, knowing his breath would send further shivers through her.

"Oh, yes." She paused, panting. "You're

not…" Her voice trailed off as he traced the bumps of her spine. "It's…it feels…I…"

"Good?"

"Yes, good…so…"

He caressed the nerve-rich center in the small of her back and her whole body convulsed.

"Oh, Sebastian! How are you…what…"

He chuckled at her incoherence.

"Not funny." Her voice was low and filled with want. "Amazing."

He smiled and kissed along her neck, tasting her sweet skin. "Surprised your body is so sensitive?"

"Yes." Her fingers dug into his neck. "I didn't know it could feel like this from you touching only my back."

"Is my princess's front feeling neglected?" he teased.

"I…" But she didn't say whatever she'd planned, merely turned her head from side to side on his shoulder as he squeezed and caressed her backside.

"Ah, Lina. You are so responsive. I want to touch you all over."

"O-okay."

Unwilling to deprive himself of the pleasure, he leaned his head forward so he could see down the front of her. Then using both hands, he peeled her wet swimsuit away from the generous curve of her breasts. Drawn into tight nubs, her dusky nipples came into view. He cupped both mouthwatering mounds, allowing his thumbs to brush over the distended nipples.

She gasped and turned her face into his neck, her body going rigid and then languid, but her grip on his nape did not falter.

He gently pinched her nipples and *she bit him.* It was so primal and unexpected that he felt himself harden in his swim trunks, aching to be out of confinement. His teeth gritted against his own desire, he continued his manipulation of her breasts and luscious nipples. He wanted to taste them so badly, but he knew if he turned her to face him, he would lose what was left of his restraint.

He knew Lina would do nothing to stop him if he stripped her and took her right here in the water. She was mindless with her pleasure and all the new sensations her body was experiencing. He was not in the habit of being the voice of reason for two people. For that matter, he was usually only too happy to take what was on offer.

But Lina wasn't like his other women. Not only was she a virgin, but she was a client. She would think sex meant happily ever after, but he didn't do permanent. Damn it, even if he was stupid enough to be tempted, she was a princess. Her father would never allow her to be with Hawk. Not short-term and not long-term. For all the independence she thought she had gained for herself at university, her father's word was law in Lina's life. Hawk could not keep her and trying would only lead to pain. Despite knowing this, he knew his control was more precarious than it had ever been.

His right hand slipped downward, traveling in

ever moving circles until his fingertips brushed the top of her bikini bottoms. He ran his index finger along her skin just inside the waistband.

She went still, her breaths ceasing.

He stopped when he was just above her never before touched mound. Then, *oh so slowly*, he allowed his hand to go beneath concealing fabric until he cupped her between her legs.

Her thighs tightened convulsively, trapping his hand where it was. "You…I…what…" Her words came out broken and breathless.

"Shh…let me touch you, Lina. It's what we both want."

"I…"

"You want me to make you feel good."

"Yes."

"Relax your legs for me, princess. Let me in."

"In?" she asked, her voice laced with sultry confusion.

"In," he commanded. He moved his fingers just enough for her to taste the pleasure to come.

"Yes…." she hissed, her legs relaxing.

He carefully pressed his middle finger against her pleasure center, rubbing just the tiniest bit against the already swollen knot of nerve endings at the top of her labia.

She cried out against his neck, her lower body bowing toward his touch.

"That's right," he praised as he drew tiny circles on her sensitized clitoris before delving below to allow one fingertip to touch just inside her, she was warm and very wet.

Her lips and teeth were working on his neck again as animalistic little sounds came from her throat.

She was so close…and he had every intention of taking her over.

Using the heel of his hand, he stimulated her pleasure button while he caressed her silky wet lips with his fingers. Increasing the pressure on her nipple, he pressed his lower body against her and felt his own pleasure rise to irretrievable levels.

They climaxed together, her scream mixing

with his primal yell in a sound that satisfied a place deep in his soul he had never even known was there.

She went limp against him, her hands falling from his neck. Only his hands kept her from slipping into the water. He felt a warm wetness on his neck that was not from the lake and her breath hitched in an unmistakable tell.

"Are you crying, my princess?" he asked.

"A little."

"Why?" Had she not been ready for this introduction to sexual pleasure?

"That was so amazing. I've never felt this close to anyone in my life. It's so good it almost hurts."

Her words acted like a falling ice glacier to his senses. Those were definitely the words of a woman looking for more than physical satiation from a man. She wanted to go into emotional waters neither one of them could navigate.

Damn it all to hell and back again.

"Hey, guys, having fun?"

Bob's voice came as an almost welcome interruption. If he could discount the fact that yet again Hawk's here-to-fore infallible reputation was at risk of being destroyed. No matter how amazing it had been.

Lina's body went rigid and he realized how exposed she must feel. He was grateful they were facing away from shore for her sake, but felt like a complete idiot in regard to his charge to protect her. In every way, he had failed. Doing the only thing he could to mitigate the damage, he gently dropped her into the water and covered her fumbling with her top by turning to face Bob. "How was the river?"

"Awesome. You two will have to try it tomorrow... unless you're still too nervous to go on moving water."

Hawk ignored the taunt. He had bigger things to worry about than that jock-boy's slur to his pride. Like the fact that Bob had made it to the lake without Hawk even noticing he was in the vicinity. Again.

What he had just done with Lina was stupid from every side. He had not built up his agency to top international status by making mistakes like this. Or any mistakes for that matter. He'd proven time and again that he was every bit the businessman that his father was without the other man's weakness when it came to women. His mother wasn't the only woman to manage a better payout than most stockholders from his father's companies. The senior Hawk had once told his son he could afford bad judgment when it came to his feminine company.

Only Hawk had always wondered how the older man's pride could stand it. He knew the two times he'd almost been taken for a ride had been enough for him and since then he'd had a perfect record.

That wasn't going to change now.

Not for Lina.

Not for anyone.

So, he'd better get his damn libido under control.

* * *

Lina played with the food on her plate, trying not to stare at Sebastian and mostly failing miserably. How could he sit there so calmly, chatting with the others after what had happened that afternoon?

Looking at him, you would never know that he'd given her the most intense and mind altering experience of her life.

Which was best. Right?

If he acted all possessive and physically affectionate, she would probably run for the hills. Emotional intimacy was not something she was used to, not to mention the physical closeness.

The truth was, the way she'd responded to Sebastian's touch scared the life out of her. Even right now, just being in the same room with him was making it hard to breathe normally, much less focus on the conversation going on around her.

He didn't seem to have any such problems.

What did that mean?

Suddenly their eyes met and the look he gave

her made her toes curl. Okay, so he was just better at masking his feelings. Which, considering the experience she had in that regard, said a lot for his self-discipline.

Which was just another thing to love about him. Um…admire. She meant admire, right? She didn't love him. Not yet. She might be falling, but she wasn't past the point of no return, was she? Oh, gosh…*was she*? Love was a truly scary emotion. When you loved people, they had the power to hurt you. Hadn't she learned that with her own family?

Echoes of the pain she'd felt when she finally realized her parents would not be coming to take her home still lingered in the deep recesses of her heart. She'd idolized her father, the king. So handsome, so powerful, so revered by everyone in Marwan. She'd adored her beautiful, always composed mother. At the age of six, she had not yet realized that her feelings of affection were not returned.

She'd missed them so much when she'd first

come to America. She'd cried herself to sleep every night, though never in front of anyone else. She'd already learned that much control by the tender age. She'd longed for her big brother and younger sister. Lina's heart had cracked more and more each day she remained in her aunt and uncle's home without her parents requesting her return until it had finally shattered on the day she'd accepted that the family that she loved did not love or need her. She'd been careful not to open her heart completely to anyone since.

Not to her aunt, who treated Lina like a gift she had never expected to have. Not to her uncle who treated her better than her father ever had. Oh, she was affectionate to them, even loved them…but not as deeply as that innocent six-year-old had loved her parents.

Out of self-preservation, she'd never let herself feel that deeply again.

Until now.

CHAPTER FOUR

LINA surged up from the table, picking up her far-from-empty plate.

"What's up, Lina-girl?" Bob asked.

"I…uh…I'm not hungry. I think I'll go for a walk."

Sebastian stood. "I'll go with you."

"No!" She took a deep breath. "I mean, finish your dinner. I feel like my own company right now." She forced a smile to mitigate the rejection.

Sebastian frowned. "It's not safe to walk in the forest alone."

Lina's roommate, Jennifer, stood. "I'm finished eating and could use a walk myself."

"Okay," Lina said quickly. In her current state,

the other woman's company was definitely preferable to Sebastian's.

And from the determined glint in his eyes, Lina had a feeling she wasn't getting out of the cabin alone. She'd spent her life coming to know what battles to fight and which ones to give in gracefully on. This situation called for partial surrender. Frankly she just wanted out of the cabin and his presence. Like now. Right this minute. Having the quiet former soldier along would not be a hardship, even if Lina *preferred* to be alone.

How many times in her almost twenty years had she been forced to choose the lesser of two evils?

Sebastian nodded his approval, like it was necessary. So, maybe not *so* different from the men in her family.

Lina immediately felt guilty for the thought. Sebastian did not treat her like a puppet without a brain.

"So, you and Sebastian a couple, or something?" Jennifer asked in her blunt manner as they stepped off the cabin's porch and headed toward the woods.

"Uh…something. I think."

"That doesn't sound like you're all that sure."

"I'm not. I'm, uh, pretty inexperienced with guys and relationships, I guess."

"Seriously? Because you could be a model or something with your exotic looks."

"Look who's talking."

Jennifer snorted. "Yeah. Plenty of guys in the military mistook me for a dumb blonde and lived to regret it."

"Tell me about it." Except the living to regret it part, though she was pretty sure that when it came to her, the king of Marwan would have a rude awakening one day.

"I bet." Jennifer looked up at the star-laden sky. "It's gorgeous out here."

"Yes, it is."

Jennifer started to go toward the lake and Lina said, "Let's go this way."

The other woman gave her a measured look in the moonlight, but obediently took a path that went in the opposite direction to the lake.

"So, does Sebastian treat you like that?"

"Like I don't have a brain in my head?"

"Yeah."

"No. In fact, he's one of the few men in my life who really listens to me and takes my opinions and thoughts seriously."

"Sounds like a good guy."

"He is."

"But you aren't sure about him?"

"Like I said, I'm pretty uneducated when it comes to the man-woman thing."

"Do you want to talk about it?"

Lina considered how odd it was that she would be having this discussion with the tough ex-soldier, but then shrugged. She'd take what she could get in the way of a friendly ear. "Love scares me," she said, surprising herself with her candor.

"You'd be pretty dumb if it didn't, in my opinion."

"People you love can hurt you."

"Even when they don't mean to." Jennifer sounded like she knew what she was talking about.

Lina sighed in agreement.

"The thing is, they can also bring more joy into your life than anyone or anything else."

Lina hadn't had a lot of experience with that. Even her beloved brother was a source of both pain and joy in her life. She missed him so much sometimes. "Really?"

"Yeah." Again that tone that said Jennifer had enough personal experience to back up what she said.

"What if he doesn't love me?"

"Sebastian?"

"Who else?"

Jennifer laughed. "Right. Falling in love is a risk, but it's one I'm not sure you can avoid. Even when you want to."

"You don't think we can control our emotions?" Lina's mother would disagree. Vehemently.

"Not when it comes to true love. If you're falling in love, the only chance you have of derailing your feelings is to not see him. And even that doesn't always work."

"I don't want to stop seeing him."

"Then I think you're screwed."

Lina was startled into a laugh. "Not yet."

"Oh? He's not pushing you too fast? That's a good sign," Jennifer said, proving she knew exactly what Lina had been thinking.

Both women burst into laughter. "I can't believe I said that," Lina gasped.

"I can." Jennifer went serious. "So, you're nervous about your feelings for Sebastian?"

"Terrified, more like."

"What scares you the most?"

"That he doesn't love me, too."

"So, you *do* love him?"

Lina bit her lip and watched the beam of her flashlight play along the forest floor. Then, she took a deep breath and nodded as she let it out. "Yes."

"I figured. You watch him the way I watch my fiancé."

"You're engaged?"

"Yes. To a national from my last posting. He's applied for a student visa and should be here with me next year."

"I bet you miss him."

"Like a lost limb. Yes."

"How did you know you were in love?"

"I couldn't imagine my life without him in it. At least not without a lot of pain."

That sounded familiar. "How did you know he loved you?"

"He told me. I mean, he showed it, too, but I'm a pretty literal person. I didn't read the signs until he admitted it out loud."

"What were the signs you didn't recognize at first?"

"The way he put my needs first."

Sebastian had certainly done that. Her experience with him that afternoon had been the most intense emotional moment of her life. The way he'd touched her had been so perfect, so unselfish.

She might lack practical experience in the relationship area, but even she knew that the way Sebastian Hawk had put her pleasure first with no thought to his own was not common.

"What else?" she asked.

"Even though I was a highly trained, not to mention tough, soldier, he was really protective toward me. He worried about me."

"Like making sure you didn't walk alone in the woods at night?" And that wasn't the only example of Sebastian's protectiveness toward her. Not by far. He seemed to have a real thing for her personal safety, always lecturing her on going out alone, walking places she should drive (in his opinion anyway).

Jennifer smiled. "Yes."

"Hmm…"

"There's the sex thing, too."

Lina stumbled at her new friend's continued bluntness. "Uh, yes, there *is* that."

"So, was it good?"

"We didn't have sex," Lina said, louder than she'd intended.

"But something *did* happen?"

"Yes."

"And?"

"It was indescribable."

"Good. Sexual compatibility is a big component to a strong relationship."

"I think maybe we're too compatible." Lina had behaved in a way she had never expected of herself. Her depth of feeling that afternoon scared her as much as the prospect of being in love with Sebastian.

"Trust me, there is no such thing as too compatible. If he makes you feel like fireworks are tame by comparison, you're a lucky woman."

"But how can I know if he felt the same?"

"Was he out of control?"

She thought of the fact that Sebastian had touched her in a semipublic place, something she was sure he would not normally do, and nodded. "To a certain extent."

"But he maintained enough control to be what you needed?"

"And then some." Lina was glad for the darkness because her cheeks were burning. "You think that means he loves me?"

"Could. You sound like you have a hard time believing it."

"I am."

"Why?"

"I, um…I'm used to being seen as who I am in reference to my family. The thought of him loving me for who I am…just plain Lina Marwan…" Not a princess from a super wealthy royal family. "It's just way outside of my usual frame of reference."

"So, you're from some really rich family, or something?"

"Yes."

"You do a good job of coming off just like any other coed."

"Thanks."

Jennifer laughed. "I guess you work at it."

"Definitely." The other woman could have no idea how difficult that feat was, either. Ditching her bodyguards was nothing compared to keeping them in the background so that no one knew she had them trailing after her all of the time.

Deep in thought, Lina followed Jennifer back to the cabin. What would happen if she told Sebastian she loved him? Was that something she was supposed to do? Or was she supposed to wait for him to declare himself? She should have listened more closely when the other girls at school talked about their adolescent relationships. At least she'd have some frame of reference.

What if Sebastian *did* love her? What did that mean for Lina and the rest of her life? She knew her parents had every intention of choosing her husband and arranging the marriage. She doubted they would even consider her opinion before negotiating the prenuptial contract on her behalf. She would be lucky to meet her future husband before the engagement was announced.

So, what would her parents do when they discovered she'd chosen her own future mate? Oh gosh. She was getting way ahead of herself. Just because Sebastian liked kissing and touching her didn't mean he saw a future together. That much she did know from listening to the other girls in school.

Sexual attraction did not equate to love. It was a lot easier to tell her brain that than to get her heart to accept it.

Regardless, the very fact that she wanted to date him was going to send her family into a tizzy. Considering the depth of her feelings for him, she didn't know how long she could keep this secret. She had more impetus to do so than ever before, but she also craved his company more than she could get away with in her current schedule of ditching her bodyguards.

Why did life have to be so complicated? She was a princess, but far from making her life easier, that status only made it almost impossible to follow her own dreams. It wasn't fair, but then she'd learned long ago that life rarely was.

Over the next few days, Sebastian showed just how in tune with her state of mind he was and how much he respected her feelings. He'd been treating her with a careful distance that helped her deal with her confused emotions and the lingering mortification she felt from almost getting caught in a hugely compromising position.

As much as she liked it, she wasn't comfortable with the overwhelming nature of her burgeoning sexuality. Remembering how wantonly she had responded to Sebastian's touch was only mitigated by her memory of the praise he'd given her for that response. The fact Bob had only missed seeing her half naked body because of Sebastian's quick action left a feeling of shame she could not quite rid herself of.

Her mother would be furious if she knew. Heck, even her more tolerant aunt would be horrifically disappointed in Lina's lack of control.

She'd talked about it to Jennifer; the woman had become a good friend in a very short time. The ex-soldier told Lina she was repressed. Lina had to agree, but she didn't know how to change that. She'd spent her entire life having it drilled into her that she had to maintain control of her emotions at all cost. Amidst the miasma of feelings besetting her, one thing had become clear to Lina: the only way to completely control her reaction to Sebastian was to stay away from him. And she wasn't willing to do that.

So, against her lifelong training, she was determined to ignore the niggles of guilt and shame that did not want to let her go. She might not be able to help the fact that she was every bit as repressed as Jennifer accused her of being, but she did not have to give into that aspect of her nature any more than she had to accept her father's view of her identity and value in life.

Part of her wished that Sebastian would push the physical intimacy, but he had been careful not to pressure her sexually. And she had to admire him for that. She really did. It would just be easier if he made the first move. Only she got the feeling he was waiting for her to decide what she wanted and then to tell him.

Despite the distance he'd maintained since the afternoon on the lake, she did not feel rejected. If anything, he spent more time with her and was attentive to her in every way, even as he kept his physical distance.

Lina had always prided herself on not being a coward. She'd taken risks over and over again to try new things, to experience life beyond the box others tried to build around her because of her status as a princess. Sebastian and the way she felt about him was definitely worth taking another risk.

She would have to make the first move and no matter how much her repressed nature cringed at that idea, she would not be cowed by personal hang-ups.

The river rushed toward Lina, growing from a ribbon in the distance to a sparkling expanse, as details from the last time she'd seen Sebastian came into focus.

Lina had arranged to meet Sebastian at Jennifer's apartment. She would have liked to use her own, but living with a traditional chape-rone chosen by her aunt made that impossible. She was not yet ready for her family to know about Sebastian and had no intention of ever di-vulging the level of intimacy she hoped to attain with him on this "date."

She'd managed to get approval for spending the night with Jennifer after her security staff ran a background check on Lina's newfound friend. She'd been shocked they agreed to leave her at the apartment without a security detail watching, but was grateful.

Jennifer, being a true friend, had made plans to be gone for the evening. Lina was free to follow through on her determination to make the next move in her relationship with Sebastian.

She had spent more time stressing over what to wear than she had planning and cooking their traditional Middle Eastern dinner. She'd given up on her current wardrobe in despair and invited Jennifer to go shopping with her.

Since the other woman knew at least some measure of truth about Lina's background, they were even able to do the shopping trip under the auspices of Lina's security team. She'd never gone shopping with a girlfriend before and found that the tough ex-soldier was in no way immune to the delights of the mall. They had spent hours trying on clothes, visiting cosmetic counters and shopping for just the right accessories.

Lina's outfit was definitely sexier than anything she had ever worn before, but it was not skanky. Or so Jennifer assured her. The thin, scoop necked silk sweater by Jones New York clung to her generous curves, as did the low-rise medium wash jeans she'd bought to go with it. She'd taken her shoes off and her bare toes peeked out from the flared hems. A belt of dark leather medallions attached with copper colored grommets rode her hips over the camel colored sweater.

Both Jennifer and the sales associate had assured Lina it was a casual, but sexy look.

The clothes were also comfortable, which was just as well since she was practically crawling out of her skin with nerves from what she planned to do.

CHAPTER FIVE

SEBASTIAN arrived only a minute, or so, after Jennifer had left. Thank goodness. Lina's stress level would never have stood up to a long wait. His knock was firm and confident. Like the man.

Lina opened the door with a smile that only felt slightly forced. "Hello, Sebastian."

He didn't smile, but she was used to that. She'd learned he did so rarely, but since she'd noticed that his smile seemed to be reserved pretty much exclusively for her, she didn't mind at all. His expression was anything but cold, though. His look practically singed her.

So, the shopping trip had been worth it.

"Hey." He looked around the small apartment. "Where's Jennifer?"

"She's not here."

"I thought we were having dinner."

"We are."

His eyes narrowed. "But not *with* Jennifer?"

"Um, no. I thought we could use some time alone."

Something flickered in his gunmetal gaze. "That's not necessary, Lina."

She bit her lip, took a deep breath and firmed her resolve. "I think it is."

He sniffed the air. "Something smells good. What are we having?"

She allowed the subject change. "I've prepared B'stellela, traditional Middle Eastern salad, apricot chicken, vegetable cous cous, braized beef kabobs and fresh mango for dessert."

"Wow. Sounds delicious. I didn't know you were such a gourmet cook."

She relaxed a little at his praise. It was only as she'd been reciting the menu that she realized he might think she'd gone overboard on it. "I'm not, but I enjoy preparing food for the people I care about."

She'd never cooked for her parents, though. Only her aunt and uncle and her brother when he came to visit. She'd even made B'stellela for her sister on occasion when she'd been in Marwan. But getting time in the palace kitchens was trickier than managing time without her bodyguards.

Sebastian's visage turned even warier and it was at that point she realized that had been his mien since arriving in the apartment. What did he have to be concerned about? Had she misread his interest in her? Hard to misread a man touching her more intimately than she'd ever been touched before, she thought. No, something else had to be making him react this way.

Or she could be misreading him completely.

Deciding they could both use a break from the tension, even if it was all in her head, she said, "Would you like something to drink before we eat?"

He made a visible effort to relax his shoulders. "Sure."

So, not in her head.

She nodded and went to pour him a glass of Absolut she'd gotten Jennifer to buy for her. "Why don't you sit down and relax with this while I put the food on the table?"

"All right." He looked down at the oversize pillows she'd set up in front of the coffee table. "Here?"

"Yes."

"So, we're going all out authentic with tonight's dinner?"

"Yes, I hope you don't mind."

"Not at all."

She hoped he still felt that way when she informed him they would be eating with their fingers just like such a meal would be consumed in Marwan.

He took a sip of his vodka and his eyes widened. "It's very strong."

"Yes. My uncle says this makes other vodkas seem like drinking water."

"You are not drinking any?" Sebastian asked with obvious displeasure at the thought of her doing so.

"Of course not." She wasn't fond of the taste of alcohol and she'd been raised to believe that setting a good example for others was of paramount importance, even for an incognito princess.

Drinking alcohol when she was not of age would certainly be considered a poor example to set.

"Good."

"Thank you, Officer Do-Right."

He had the grace to look chagrined. "I'm sorry. I did not mean to sound like your father."

"My father would assume I would never consider drinking a man's beverage, but my brother would question me."

A faint smile creased Sebastian's features. "Then I apologize for sounding like your brother."

"Do not worry, Sebastian. I do not in any way think of you like my brother." She did not wait to see his response to that bit of honesty, but beat a hasty retreat to the kitchen.

He was putting his glass down after taking what looked like a hefty drink when she returned with the B'stellela. She set the pastry covered in powdered sugar and stuffed with egg, lamb and cooked vegetables down on the low table before lowering herself to the cushion beside him. Then she lifted the silver water pot over the bowl for finger washing.

He must have been to the Middle East at some point or at least dined at an authentic restaurant because he put his hands out for her to run the water over without hesitation. He then returned the favor for her and they both dried their hands on the tea towels she'd placed at either side of the silver bowl.

She pinched off a piece of the stuffed pastry and lifted it to his lips. "Taste."

Something dark moved in his eyes and he

opened his lips for her to feed him. His tongue brushed her fingers as he took the bite.

Sharp tingles of electric charge arced up her arm and she gasped, her gaze locked with his.

"It's very good."

"Thank you."

She fed him another bite. He looked like he was going to refuse it, but at the last second his mouth opened again. Once more she felt the velvet tip of his tongue. Oh, man. No wonder Jennifer had recommended feeding each other. It was incredibly erotic.

"I can feed myself," he said when he finished chewing.

"But I like feeding you." She really did. She'd never done anything like this before and she liked it as much as the other new things she had experienced with him. It was all so wonderfully intimate. It made her feel close to him…like she belonged with him.

He seemed to have an internal battle and then he took another sip of his drink. He put the glass down again and took a pinch of the phyllo pastry. "You will have to allow me to return the favor."

She nodded, her mouth suddenly too dry for speech.

He presented the bite to her lips and she took it, tasting the spicy saltiness of his fingers as a subtle flavor under that of the sweet-savory pastry. She sucked his fingertips as he slowly withdrew them from her mouth.

He groaned. "You don't know what you are doing to me, Lina."

"I hope I do," she whispered.

He looked pained, but took another bit of pastry to feed her. She did the same and they fed each other simultaneously.

"I shouldn't be doing this," he said in an agonized voice after the third such synchronous bite.

"It's all right, Sebastian." She brushed his lower lip with her forefinger. "This is right."

He shook his head, but just swallowed rather than saying anything.

"Would you like some more vodka?" she asked softly.

"No. I definitely should not drink any more of that witch's brew."

She giggled. "Oh, my uncle would be so offended at that description."

"Are you going to tell him?"

"No."

"I've never met your family." He said it casually, but for Lina it was anything but an indifferent topic.

"Do you want to meet them?"

"I just think it is interesting that I have never met anyone from your family as much time as we spend together. For me, there's just my dad and he lives on the East Coast. But you've mentioned your brother, sister, parents and your aunt and uncle."

"None of them live near the university."

"You live alone then?"

"Uh, no…I've got a roommate." That was one description for her chaperone. "She's terribly nosy. That's why we're having dinner here rather than in my apartment."

"I see."

She doubted it. Few people had to tolerate the level of intrusion into the privacy of their life as royalty, but that was the cost of being who she was. Or so she'd been told over and over again since birth. She shook off the thought and smiled. "Are you ready for the salad?"

"Salad is good."

She took the remaining pastry away and returned with the salad and a small bowl of bread pieces. They fed each other again, but the traditional salad was messy and they ended up laughing more than anything else. She served the three elements of the main dish together on a single oblong platter with the two meats on each side and the cous cous in the center.

The apricot chicken was sweet and tangy, and for the first time in the hundreds of times she'd eaten it, it had a strangely aphrodisiaclike quality. Or something did because this time when bits of the sauce dribbled onto his chin, all she wanted to do was lick them off...not laugh. Not even sort of.

It seemed to affect him the same way because he actually leaned toward her before groaning and wiping at something at the corner of her mouth with his thumb.

"This is my favorite meal, but I have never enjoyed eating it as much as right now," she admitted in a voice laced with awe she made no attempt to stifle.

She didn't mind him knowing he had such a profound impact on her.

His eyes devoured her with such intensity that her body shook. His jaw tightened, but he said nothing.

"It's the company," she dared to say, leaning just slightly forward.

A strangled sound came from his throat and he jumped up. "I need to..." His voice trailed off as he headed to the bathroom.

Deflated, Lina slumped on her seating

cushion. Maybe she'd been wrong. Maybe Sebastian *didn't* want her. At least not anymore. Had her reaction in the lake disgusted him, but he'd been too polite to say so? Only it seemed that he had been trying very hard to get exactly the response she had given him.

Bits of lectures from both her mother and her aunt rang in Lina's ears, condemning her embracing her newfound sensuality. She looked down at her clothes and noticed that in her current sitting position the shadowed valley between her breasts was on display. Feeling the disappointed gaze of both her mother and her aunt even though the women were miles—and in the case of her mother an ocean—away, she yanked the top up, covering the cleavage.

Then she stumbled to her feet, her limbs still suffering the effects of arousal. Quickly clearing the low table of food, she silently berated herself for foolishly believing she and Sebastian had something special.

Something he wanted to keep and explore as much as she did.

He came out of the bathroom as she put dessert on the table, this time with forks to eat it with. She wasn't risking making an idiot of herself again. She'd poured two glasses of sweetened mint tea as well and placed them beside the dessert bowls as Sebastian sat down.

Instead of taking her place beside him, she took a position on the sofa across the coffee table from him.

His brows rose in question, but she ignored the silent communication. If he wasn't going to verbalize the question, she wasn't going to embarrass herself by answering it.

"Are you all right, Lina?"

"Fine." She took a bite of mango that tasted like sawdust in her mouth.

"Why are you sitting up there?"

Oh, now that was just mean. Like he didn't know. She frowned at him. "I felt like it."

His expression was pained. "I see."

"I'm sure you do." She looked down at her dessert and asked, "Would you prefer coffee to the mint tea?"

"I would prefer you were sitting beside me again."

"Right."

"Damn it, Lina."

Her head came up and she glared into his eyes. "What? I got the message, all right? I can't help it if I need the physical distance. Pointing it out is hardly tactful and it would be a kindness if you would simply drop the subject right now. It won't happen again, I assure you."

"What won't happen?" He looked genuinely confused and not a little frustrated himself. "Nothing *has* happened."

Her attempted seduction was nothing? That was an even more demoralizing thought than what her family would think of her behavior. "Right. *Nothing important* has occurred here tonight."

He said an ugly word and she flinched.

"I apologize," he muttered.

They ate in silence, neither one finishing their fruit before pushing the bowls away. She took the cue and got up to clear the table, forgoing the final ceremonial hand washing after dinner. He'd obviously done so when he was in the bathroom and she'd washed her hands in the kitchen sink when she was clearing the main course. Since they'd used forks, they didn't need to do so again and she wanted to avoid any semblance of additional intimacy.

So many thoughts and feelings were rushing through her that she couldn't make sense of any of them. She didn't know if his hasty retreat to the bathroom was an all-out rejection, or not.

Sebastian stood and helped her carry dishes and cutlery into the kitchen. She filled the sink with water and soap to wash the dishes. She'd planned to do it later, but now she needed something to keep her hands occupied.

He joined her at the sink and began rinsing the

dishes as she placed them in the second sink, then drying them.

"You don't need to help. This will only take me a minute." She'd washed all the cooking utensils before he arrived.

"I don't mind."

She stifled a sound of annoyance. She needed a break from his presence, but he seemed singularly obtuse to that fact.

"These are beautiful dishes," he said. "Are they yours?"

"Yes." They were from the traditional set of china her aunt had given her when she moved into the apartment with her chaperone.

"Are they family heirlooms?"

"Not heirlooms, I don't think, but they're from my family's home country."

"Where is that?"

"Marwan."

"Like your last name."

"Yes."

"That's pretty interesting."

"I guess." She wasn't telling him all her secrets, especially tonight of all nights.

"Is it a common name in your country?"

"Not too common, no."

"Does that mean you are someone special in your country?"

"*My* country is the United States, but if you mean Marwan…no, I'm really no one special there." Not special enough to keep around, not important enough to have a voice in her family or anything else.

"You sound angry."

"No." Sad and disappointed by that reality, but not angry. Not anymore.

His hands on her shoulders, he turned her to face him. "Look at me."

She shook her head, her gaze firmly fixed on his chest. Which was not conducive to her peace of mind, but it was better than meeting his eyes.

He tipped her chin up. "Lina."

"What?"

"Tell me what is bothering you."

"Please, Sebastian, drop it."

His thumb brushed over her lips. "I can't." And he sounded really bothered by that fact.

She bit back a whimper at his touch. "I know that you don't want me. And that's okay. Really. I just. I feel stupid."

"Stupid? Oh not stupid, princess. Never that. If anything, you are too intelligent."

Not believing the compliment for a minute, she shrugged. As she did so, she realized that somehow he'd moved even closer because her breasts brushed against his upper abs. Her nipples tightened against the silk sweater. If he looked down, he could not miss the evidence of her weakness. She prayed he did not look down.

"Why do you think I don't want you?"

"I can't believe you are asking me that. Do we have to talk about this, Sebastian? You may not have feelings for me, but I thought we were at least friends. Why would you want to humiliate me?" she asked, unable to keep the tears fighting to break free out of her voice.

His hand on her shoulder tightened. "The last thing I want to do is humiliate you."

"Then maybe you should go in the other room." She swallowed. "Before I humiliate myself."

"You want me."

"You can't doubt that after the afternoon at the lake."

"I could say the same."

"I'm not the one who jumped up and ran to the bathroom when we almost kissed…and it's not as if you've done anything since the kayaking trip. I thought at first you were giving me space, letting me come to terms with my feelings, but now I realize you simply didn't want anything more from me…that way, I mean." Tears she'd been battling since before dessert broke free and trickled down her cheeks.

He closed his eyes. "Don't cry, princess."

"I'm not." She didn't even blush at the blatant lie.

His eyes opened and met hers. "You really don't think I want you?"

She sniffed, blinking away the moisture from her eyes. "It's obvious. Can we stop talking about this now?"

"Yes, we can stop talking now." Then with a groan that sounded like a dam breaking, his mouth smashed down on hers, his lips taking possession of hers with passion that felt both angry and desperate, but most of all…genuine.

He broke the kiss and rested his forehead against hers, his breath coming in gasps as ragged as her own. "I don't want to hurt you, sweetheart."

"Wanting me hurts me?" she asked in confusion.

"There are reasons this thing between us can't go anywhere."

"What reasons?" Then not even waiting for an answer, she said, "No, I don't believe you. That's a copout. I've been told all my life there are reasons I can't pursue my dreams, but I fought then and I'm willing to fight now. To fight for us."

"You can't always fight."

"I don't believe that…unless…are you married?"

He barked out a harsh laugh. "No."

"Engaged?"

"No."

"Seriously involved, or committed to someone else?"

"No."

"Then whatever you think this insurmountable obstacle is, we can overcome it."

"You don't understand."

"So, make me understand. After." With that she kissed him, not willing to listen to him tell her why they shouldn't want each other. It was enough that they did.

He was perfect for her and she would convince him that she was just right for him.

If she'd thought his initial kiss was volatile, it was nothing compared to his response now. He literally lifted her off her feet, pressing her body tightly against his as his mouth ate at hers in a devouring so hot, her lips felt like they were on fire.

He was moving, but she couldn't make herself care where they were going. When her back hit the wall, she merely tightened her hold on his shoulders. Her legs spread of their own volition, making room for him in an invitation she'd never offered before but which felt wholly natural. He was quick to accept, maneuvering her so that his steel-hard erection pressed directly against the apex of her thighs. Sparks of pleasure shot through her and she moaned.

"You're killing me," he growled against her ear before nipping at the tender lobe and then laving it with his tongue.

She couldn't get her mouth to form words, so she let her body answer for her, undulating against him as much as she could considering her position between his big, hard body and the equally unforgiving wall.

He licked along her neck, sending shivers all through her. "You taste so good."

"Better than dinner?" she managed to tease. Go her.

"Better than anything," he ground out in a voice that held no amusement, only pure male animal hunger.

How had she gone her whole life without feeling this way even once before? But the answer was obvious. She had not yet met Sebastian Hawk and no one else could or would make her feel this good…this needed. The tension was building inside her again…like it had at the lake. She could feel the overwhelming pleasure climbing toward the inevitable peak, but she wasn't ready for it.

She wasn't ready for this to end and she wanted to bring Sebastian pleasure, too. She knew he'd found his release at the lake, or at least she thought that was what his shout had meant, but she wanted to see him this time.

To see his face in the throes of passion beyond his control. She needed that.

An annoying beep tried to impinge on her

consciousness, but she ignored it in favor of touching Sebastian's neck and back, mapping and memorizing the play of his sculpted muscles under her fingertips.

With a curse, he suddenly let her go and stepped away from her as he fumbled for the phone in his pocket.

CHAPTER SIX

SHE tried to burrow back into his arms, but he shook his head, a look of disgust on his face as he pushed her away.

Hurt and confusion at his blatant rejection mixed with the cauldron of emotions churned up by his kiss and she slumped against the wall.

He turned away from her and flipped his phone open. "Hawk here."

How could he sound so dispassionate after what they'd just been doing?

He was silent for several seconds as he listened to his caller speak. Then he turned back to face her, his face set in impassive lines. "So, the threat has been neutralized and my assignment here is done?"

Another silence while he listened, this one much shorter.

"My final report will be ready the day after tomorrow. I have several recommendations for more effective security."

Another layer of confusion clouded Lina's brain as she tried to make sense of Sebastian's conversation in light of who she knew him to be.

"Right, arrange with my assistant for a time to meet and I'll present the report in person."

Another short silence.

Sebastian said, "I'll be on the first flight out tomorrow."

He said something else and flipped the phone shut.

Trembling and a feeling of nausea growing, she swallowed against the dryness in her throat. "Flight out? Where are you going?"

He grimaced, as if the conversation was distasteful, but other than that no emotion showed in his expression. "I'm returning to my home office tomorrow."

"Home office? I thought you were a graduate student."

"That was my cover."

"Cover? Are you an FBI agent, or something?" She didn't know how well she would handle having a relationship with someone who had a job like that. It *would* explain why he had hesitated to take their relationship to a deeper level, though.

"Or something."

"What?"

His hands fisted at his sides, but that was the only indication he was uncomfortable with this conversation. "I own an international investigation and security firm that specializes in the high end market."

Lina's stomach cramped as a suspicion started to form. "You mean like catering to royalty?"

"Some. Hawk Investigations has a clientele predominately comprised of the extremely wealthy."

"I see." But she didn't and wasn't at all sure she wanted to.

"Do you?" he asked sardonically.

"I don't know," she admitted.

"Your family received death threats and it was decided you needed additional security. It was your uncle's idea, that rather than pulling you out of university until the threat was neutralized they hire additional protection."

"Someone threatened my aunt and uncle?" she asked, fear for their safety lacing her voice.

"No, your father. Each of his children was named as a potential causality if he did not change his stance on a certain political agenda."

"Why wasn't I told? Why the cloak-and-dagger?"

"Since your studies weren't to be interrupted, it was felt that apprising you of the situation would do you more harm than good." Sebastian's voice was even, expressing no emotion whatsoever.

And she didn't know how he managed that. She felt like he'd taken a tazer to her heart. Heaven knew it hurt so bad, she didn't know how it kept beating.

"You mean my father thinks I'm so weak minded that if I had known about the threats, I would not have been able to keep my attention on my studies." She said with a bitterness for more than the paternal arrogance.

"His head of security did not tell me the details of the motivation behind their decision to make your added protection clandestine."

"You just do what you're told, right?" Well, this explained why her security men had allowed her to spend the night at Jennifer's without hanging around. They knew she was already being watched.

"That's my job."

"And you always do your job without voicing an opinion," she said with sarcasm. She refused to believe Sebastian was anybody's yes-man, even her father's.

"I agreed with the stipulation. If my agents and I were simply added to your security detail, we would have gained nothing but extra bodies between you and the threat, but by maintaining the appearance of friendship and or complete invisibility we were able to watch not only you, but your security detail as well."

"What, you thought one of them might be a traitor?"

"It's been known to happen."

She couldn't argue that. Didn't even want to. Didn't want to keep talking at all. There was too much pain inside of her and it was going to find its way out soon. "So, everything was a big deception. You weren't my friend…my anything."

"The deception was necessary."

"No, it wasn't." Pain lanced through her, but she wasn't going to let *that* comment slide. "You could have told *me* the truth."

Except it was obvious he agreed with her family that she wasn't smart or strong enough to be kept in the loop on what was happening in her own life. She felt like an idiot all right, but for trusting Sebastian. Maybe her family was right…she certainly hadn't shown good judgment of character when it came to him.

Heck, she'd let herself fall in love with a man who was lying to her in order to do his job.

"You lied to me, over and over," she whispered the accusation, the vise on her heart squeezing tighter. "I fell for you and it was all a lie. Everything."

"*I* lied?" he asked with clear censure. "And you have been so up front and honest with me, *princess*."

For the first time, the word did not sound like an endearment.

She stared at him, grateful for the wall at her back. She was sure her legs would not support her otherwise. "What were all those questions about? *Do you live alone? Why haven't I met your family?*" she mocked. "My gosh, you probably know more about my life than I do." Her voice was rising to a dangerous register. For the first time in her life, she was nearly shouting. "I thought you liked me for *me*, not because of my family's wealth or position. I can't believe how stupid I've been."

"Stop acting like the injured innocent, Lina." His voice was ice-cold. "You say you fell for me, but you never once told me the truth about yourself. I gave you a chance tonight to be honest, to trust me and you sidestepped it. Just like you have every other opportunity since we met."

"I didn't want where I come from to prejudice your opinion of me," she cried out. "Besides, the fewer people aware of my true identity, the less a security risk to me. *You* should understand that."

"That might have flown in the beginning, but we've known each other for weeks. You planned to offer me your body tonight, but intended to continue to withhold the truth. If you had *feelings* for me, you would not consider me a security risk. You certainly don't mind circumventing other measures meant to protect you when you find it convenient."

"It's not the same, *everything* about you is a lie. I do…did…care about you, but there was no relationship on your side. Just a job." Didn't he understand how much that hurt her? How wrong that was? But then, like her father, Sebastian obviously believed the ends justified the means.

For just a second, the blank mask slipped and anger blazed out of his dark gray eyes. "Just like a woman to have a double standard about honesty. You are like every other woman I have known Princess Lina bin Fahd al Marwan. Your protestations of heartfelt emotion carry as much weight as the other *truths* you have chosen to share with me."

"That's not fair, Sebastian. I had my reasons."

"Like you have your reasons for lying to your family and your security team. Does it matter to you that the men on your detail will most likely lose their jobs once my report is filed with your father's head of security? Did you once consider your family or the poor saps responsible for your safety when you were busy lying to them all so you could have *your freedom*?"

She couldn't breathe. He didn't know her at

all. She'd thought he'd understood her, but that was just another deception. However, it wasn't that knowledge that was shredding her heart right now. The men in her security detail weren't bad. They had lives, families…she could not stand to see them fired.

"You can't file a report that gets them in trouble." She didn't care if she sounded like she was begging. She was. She'd never do it on her own behalf, but for *the good of* men who relied on her family's goodwill for their livelihood she would not let her pride stand in the way.

"You should have considered that before learning to circumvent the security measures your family had put in place."

"I didn't know I was being watched by a second detail, did I? I would never have done anything to get them into trouble."

"And you don't think that if something happened to you on one of the numerous occasions you'd managed to ditch your bodyguards that they wouldn't have been fired? Or worse?"

"No one knows who I am here. I'm not at risk."

"You're beyond naïve if you believe that."

So, just like every other man in her life, Sebastian thought she was lacking brainpower. So much for his earlier comment on her intelligence. She didn't have the time to worry about that right now however. "Please, Sebastian, you can't file that report."

"I don't have a choice. I take my job seriously."

She looked down at the floor, hugging herself for comfort that was never there. She had to convince him to keep some things out of that report. "What if I promised not to do it again?"

"Not to do what exactly?"

She thought quickly before speaking, knowing that she would feel compelled to keep any promise she made to the letter. No matter what *he* thought of her honor. "What if I promised not to do any of the things that I've done to ditch my bodyguards again?"

He snorted and her head snapped up. "What?"

Then she answered her own question before he could. "You don't think I'm capable of keeping a promise."

"Like you kept your promise to be honest with your security team?"

"I've never made such a promise. I've never even claimed such a thing. It is not my fault they assume I'm too dumb or docile, or both, to arrange for a slice of personal freedom in my life."

He still looked unconvinced.

It shouldn't surprise her, but it did…and it hurt. "Look, even if our supposed friendship was nothing but smoke and mirrors, you must know me well enough by now to realize I would never do anything intentionally to hurt someone else, particularly the people dependent on me for their livelihood."

"Yet, you put the jobs of your entire security team and your chaperone at risk, not to mention your uncle losing face with your father once it comes to light that he is ignorant of big chunks of your life."

"*I never thought I would be caught.* It wasn't on purpose."

He shook his head.

"Please, Sebastian."

"You promise me you won't lie to your security detail or your family again nor will you argue against the new measures and I will consider making suggestions for your increased security without revealing why I think they are necessary."

"I promise." She certainly wasn't going to want the freedom to try dating again for a very long time. She never wanted to hurt like this again.

"I promise not to deceive my family or re-tainers when it comes to my personal security," she clarified.

She wasn't promising never to withhold the truth from her family again. She lived a whole life that they would never understand, particu-larly the little detail that she was now an American citizen.

His look anything but approving, Sebastian nevertheless nodded. "Agreed."

He refused to leave until Jennifer returned and another bodyguard had been called to watch Lina's friend's building.

It was all Lina could do to keep it together in front of him. The only way she could even remotely manage the pain was to pretend he wasn't there and pretend her mother was. It would probably seem childish to someone else, but Lina had never cried in front of her mother—at least in her memory.

The mere thought of her mother witnessing her ignomious rejection was enough to keep external tears at bay. It didn't decrease her emotional agony, though. In fact, the idea that her mother might be aware of Sebastian's employment and the nature of his cover for a way into her life intensified Lina's sense of utter betrayal. She might not be crying on the outside, but her heart was crying tears of blood.

* * *

Lina's bungee cord bottomed out and her hands brushed the water before the ricochet snapped her up again. She flipped her torso up and started undoing her harness before the final bouncing stopped. Diving into the water on the next downward plunge, she immediately started swimming for shore. She couldn't believe Sebastian was back.

He was no longer simply the hands-on owner of the largest detective and security agency in the world, but ran his deceased father's business holdings as well. Not to mention chairing multiple nonprofit boards. She had a hard time comprehending that even her father had the power to command the personal attention of business tycoon Sebastian Hawk on a case.

She was *not* surprised the king of Marwan had engaged Hawk Investigations when rather than accept the edict she marry a man she had never met, his recalcitrant daughter disappeared. After all, hadn't the agency done a bang-up job eight years ago? Not only had

Sebastian kept her safe, but he had recommended certain changes in her security that had severely limited her ability to have a life outside of her studies.

Thank goodness for Jennifer. Without her, Lina's remaining years at the university would have been miserable. Once those years were over, however, it had been those same security measures that spawned her first all-out rebellion against her family. That rebellion had resulted in a relaxation of the strictures surrounding her, but it had also led to a near break between her parents and her aunt and uncle. Once again dismissing Lina's own will and intellect, the royal couple blamed the Americanized relatives for their daughter's unwillingness to conform.

Yet despite her insistence on a certain amount of autonomy, her parents had still assumed she would be willing to marry a man of their choosing. The level of their sheer arrogance left her breathless. Then and now.

She reached the shore.

"Awesome jump, Lina. You ready to go again?" Aaron slapped her on the back…or was it Adam? She couldn't remember. He was ground crew, that's all she knew for sure.

She shook her head. "I'm going to have to forgo any more jumps today. Can someone give me a ride back to the hotel? Um…right away?"

She wasn't naïve enough to believe she could outrun Sebastian, but she definitely didn't want to have the coming confrontation in front of a group of strangers.

"You okay? Something happen on the jump?"

She shook her head. More like *someone*. "I'm fine. I just need to get back to the hotel."

"Hey, no problem. I'll take you," he said with a flirtatious smile before calling out his plans to the other ground crew.

The Jeep ate up the miles between the jump site and Lina's hotel.

Aaron…Adam…whatever…downshifted and took a tight curve coming out of the canyon on squealing tires. "So, you going back to the hotel…it got anything to do with the suit yelling his head off on the bridge?"

"Sebastian doesn't yell."

"Artie said the guy's got a set of lungs on him. Near to made Artie jump off the bridge when he pulled the gun."

"He pulled a gun?" Lina asked with genuine shock.

"Yeah, but you'd already jumped. The guy… Sebastian you said…he cursed better'n any sergeant Artie ever had in the Army, he said."

"How do you know?"

"Artie called from the bridge when the guy took off in his car. Thought he might be headed down to us."

"He might have been." But even Sebastian couldn't drive the distance by road as fast as she had plunged on her bungee cord.

She was however slightly surprised they hadn't run into each other at the junction out of the canyon.

"This Sebastian dude your boyfriend, or something?"

"Or something."

When she didn't elaborate, her blond driver just shrugged. "Hey, I can respect your privacy."

"Thank you."

"You want me to tell Artie you won't be taking the job with the outfit after all?"

Startled by the blonde's perception, she said, "If you don't mind."

"No problem. You going to need transportation into the city?"

Seeing a sleek black Jaguar parked outside her room as they pulled into the small hotel's parking lot, Lina's spine stiffened. "No, I don't think that will be necessary, but thanks for the offer."

The Jeep came to a stop beside the Jaguar. "Looks like your 'or something' beat us here. You want me to come in with you?"

Lina couldn't help smiling at that. There were lots of good people left in the world and she had to remember that. Even if her own family was happy to sell her out to the god of political expedience.

She turned to face him and put her hand on his arm. "Thanks, Aaron—"

"Adam."

She grimaced. "Sorry."

"No problem."

"I really appreciate the offer, but I'll be fine. Sebastian's not here to hurt me." Not physically anyway.

"Good luck with your life, Lina. You ever want a job, you come on back. Artie is plenty impressed with you. I am, too." There was no mistaking the interest in Adam's eyes, but Lina felt no responding feminine pique.

She hadn't felt anything like that since the night eight years ago when she discovered she was nothing but a job to Sebastian Hawk. Goodness knew she'd tried, but it was as if her libido had turned off and she had no idea how to turn it back on.

In some ways, her lack of sexual interest in

the men who had dated her had made life easier. She hadn't gotten hurt again and she'd had more time and energy to devote to her causes than she would have otherwise.

She leaned forward and kissed Adam on the cheek. "Thanks."

He turned his head and kissed her back—on the lips. He wasn't aggressive and she didn't feel threatened, but she didn't feel anything else, either. Nevertheless, she smiled before grabbing her pack from the backseat, where she'd left it that morning, and got out of the Jeep.

Sebastian was waiting in the open door to her room when she turned from the still running four-wheel drive. He was indeed wearing a suit, or at least what was left of one. He'd discarded the jacket and tie, having rolled the sleeves of his crisp white shirt up to reveal his tanned, muscular forearms. His no doubt designer label slacks had been tailored to fit his hips and long legs perfectly.

Lina's mouth watered while her hands itched to reach out and touch.

What was happening to her?

She'd spent eight years as close to asexual as a woman could get and all of a sudden her hormones were on a roller coaster that rivaled the scariest ride at Six Flags Amusement Park.

It took all of her training in hiding her emotion, to maintain a blank expression as she faced the man who had haunted her dreams for almost a decade. "Hello, Sebastian."

His left brow lifted sardonically. "You don't sound surprised to see me."

She shrugged, as if the very sight of him wasn't sending a plethora of signals to nerve endings she hadn't been aware of in eight years. "I could say the same. I could have run."

"I would have caught you."

"Probably." Her initial flight hadn't been well planned after all…more an act of rebellion than anything else. She had nothing in place to help her disappear with a hunter like Sebastian seeking her out.

That did not mean she *couldn't* disappear. Just not right this minute.

He stepped back into the room, indicating she should join him. She went without argument. Why not? Privacy was exactly what she wanted for their upcoming discussion. It also didn't hurt to lull him into believing she was as docile as her family believed she should be.

A quick double honk behind her had her turning and waving off Adam as he drove away.

Sebastian closed the door, turning the security lock as well. "I'm glad to see you being so reasonable."

"You expected anything less?" she asked, trying to ignore the sense of the room being too small now that he was in it.

"I have personal experience with how little credence you give duty to your family and crown. I admit, I expected a lot more trouble from you. You didn't even try to get your boyfriend to rescue you."

The words hurt, but she refused to let him see

that. The truth was that his opinion shouldn't matter. The fact that it had the ability to impact her made her furious…with herself. "Perhaps I don't buy into the belief that my filial duty extends to marrying a man I have never met and moreover one who has been dubbed the *Playboy Prince*. That does not mean I'm interested in getting an innocent bystander embroiled in my situation."

"I see the years have not changed you."

"Really? In what way?" she asked in masochistic compulsion.

"You are still putting your own comfort above that of the people who depend on you."

"Oh, right…because the people of Marwan are going to be devastated if I don't marry the younger son of a neighboring sheikhdom."

"Your father believes it is best for his country."

"Maybe it is, but since Marwan stopped being *my* country more than two decades ago, I fail to see why I should sacrifice my life for political expedience."

"You are still a princess in Marwan."

She shrugged, not willing to continue the argument standing there in nothing more than a damp T-shirt and shorts over her still wet swimsuit. "As fascinating as this discussion is, I need to take a shower and put some dry clothes on."

Hawk watched Lina disappear into the small bathroom, her hands filled with clothes she'd pulled from the drawer of the cheap dresser that also served as a television stand. The room had a window, but it was too small for even Lina to get through. Though he wasn't taking any chances.

"Leave the door open," he ordered.

She didn't answer, but she also didn't close the door.

Damn. He almost wanted her to disobey...to argue. So, he could have the pleasure of subduing her? What the hell was the matter with him?

And what was up with her? The Lina he remembered was not this acquiescent. He'd said she hadn't changed, but the truth was—she had. He didn't like it, which made no sense.

The fact that she made no attempt to run, or involve her blond boyfriend in trying to get rid of Sebastian was the behavior of a docile woman. His princess was anything but that. Or at least she had been eight years ago.

One thing hadn't changed in all that time. The reaction of his body to her presence. He'd had a hard-on since she climbed out of the Jeep and it was only getting more urgent as his senses took in the sounds and smells of her showering.

CHAPTER SEVEN

SHE used the same shampoo and body wash she had when they first met. The scents were unmistakable. He could hear the splashes of water as she washed herself and damned if he didn't want to strip off his own clothes and join her. This was not the way he'd planned to react to her when he agreed to take the missing persons case personally.

Her father was angry and not a little worried at Lina's disappearance. In an unprecedented move, the king had come to Hawk's office. His security advisor had accompanied him, but the king had done all the talking, practically begging Hawk to find his daughter.

Seeing another proud man brought to this

point had moved Hawk, but he was too honest with himself to pretend that was all that had influenced his decision to come after Lina. He'd never forgotten the weeks he'd spent guarding her. There were still nights he woke up with the scent of her skin a memory so real he reached for her in the bed.

She was never there, and never would be, but he had to be the one to bring her in. To deliver her to her family to marry the *Playboy Prince*. Okay, so he didn't understand why King Fahd bin Latif had arranged Lina's marriage to a sheikh who didn't seem able to keep his scandals out of the newspaper, but it wasn't Hawk's job to judge the actions of his clients.

He'd taken on an assignment and he would see it to completion.

And maybe he'd get the chance to have the conversation she had denied him the last night they saw each other and one attempt he'd made via the phone since.

He owed Lina an apology, maybe even an explanation. If he could go back, he wouldn't change his actions—at least not that he'd walked away. He'd had no choice. Her place in the royal family of Marwan dictated that reality. However he would have been more honest with her after the first kiss, instead of relying on self-control that had turned out to be weaker than he thought.

He also would have explained that his attraction to her had not been a deception, but the real deal. That even if they couldn't have a future he would rather part as friends. But he'd been totally disgusted with himself and his failure to control his libido. He'd taken it out on her, being cold and judgmental—he'd had to try and keep control—when he should have been apologizing.

A part of him had realized it then and that had only made it worse.

He found himself doing it again today. He'd been livid watching her kiss that damn water bunny and had expressed his anger in disdain he wasn't sure he even felt.

He'd taken on a job and he would see it to completion, but was it really such a bad thing for a twenty-first century woman to want to choose her own husband. Even a princess?

The sound of the shower curtain sliding back had Hawk's head snapping up. He looked through the cracked open door, knowing he would not see anything. Lina would no doubt finish dressing behind the door.

Only he hadn't taken the vanity mirror into consideration. The open door had stopped it from steaming up and the reflective surface gave a perfect mirror image of Lina drying her delectable little body. He should turn away, he knew he should. But he couldn't make himself do it.

She was so beautiful. Her honey colored skin glistened with moisture where she had not yet reached with the towel. Droplets of water dripped off the ends of her hair to roll down her generous breasts, some curving around her beaded nipples, others rolling right over the tips.

He wanted to go in there and lick those drops of water right off her and had even taken two steps forward before he caught himself. He stood rigid, locking his muscles into immobility and watching with uncontrollable fascination as she continued to dry off. She turned and bent over, exposing her heart shaped backside and the shadow of her most feminine place.

He groaned.

She stilled. "Did you say something, Sebastian?"

"Uh…no." If he didn't move, she was going to catch him watching her like an adolescent getting his first peek at a female body.

Gritting his teeth, he shut his eyes and forced himself to turn away and take several steps toward where he knew the bed was. He opened his eyes once he felt the bed against his shin. He sat down and only considered the lack of wisdom in choosing this particular spot once he was already there.

Once she came out of the bathroom, he was

not going to toss her onto the bed and ravish her within an inch of her life...or his. *He wasn't.*

Lina dressed quickly, but clothing herself acted as no barrier between her and the feelings that Sebastian elicited in her. The shower hadn't helped, either. The feel of hot water cascading over her body had acted as a catalyst to sensations she had long ago given up on.

This was so incredibly wrong.

She'd dated several men since graduating from college, men *worthy* of her affection and desire. And felt nothing for any of them.

Then Mr. Sebastian Hawk walks back into her life and within milliseconds she's reacting to him as if he'd never been away, had never betrayed her.

Sebastian had used her once and she had no intention of falling for him again. But then what she was feeling right now had nothing to do with love. It was one hundred percent physical. It had to be. There was nothing left over from her love for Sebastian. She'd loved a lie anyway. It wasn't as if anything about the man had been real eight years ago.

And she could keep reminding herself of that important truth, but it wasn't going to do a darn thing to dampen the fire lit deep inside her. Which just proved that it *was* entirely carnal in origin. Her emotions knew better than to react to the man's presence.

Apparently her body wasn't quite as wise.

She pulled her long hair up into a ponytail. She could barely see the highlights while it was wet, but dry it glinted with blond, red and light brown streaks mixed with her natural black. Her mother hated it. Her aunt loved it and Lina liked it enough to have her roots touched up every six weeks.

Wondering what Sebastian would think of it dry and trying to ignore the traitorous thought, she walked out of the bathroom. He was sitting on the bed, a pained expression on his face.

"You all right?" she asked begrudgingly.

The blank mask she'd learned to hate the night she discovered his duplicity settled over his features. "Fine. You ready to go?"

"Go where exactly?"

"Playing word games with me, Princess?"

"No. I assume you plan to deliver me to my family, but considering the fact that we are twenty-six hundred miles from D.C. and at least a four-hour drive from any sort of municipal airport, I'm assuming we've got at least one stop between here and there."

"I didn't say your family was in the States."

"You didn't have to. My father may think I'm incapable of keeping up with world events, but I'm not. Nor am I oblivious. The fact that the king of Marwan and his entourage are currently staying in our nation's capital is hardly a state secret." And if he thought he was taking her to Marwan, he was delusional.

"You're right. Your parents, not to mention your fiancé, are waiting for your arrival in D.C."

"I assume they are staying at the Embassy?"

Her father was fanatical about security and did not trust hotels or even U.S. government provided housing. The Marwan Embassy was large enough to not only house him and the royal entourage, but had several more guest rooms besides all the ordinary facilities for hosting other government dignitaries.

"Yes."

"So?"

He looked a question at her.

"Where exactly are we going now?"

"You think I should tell you?"

"I get that you fall in with my father's draconian belief that he should be able to dictate my future as well as who I share it with, but are you so tyrannical that you don't think you perhaps owe me the most basic of courtesies? Namely telling me where I should expect to spend the night?"

"Knowledge is power, Princess, and I'm not in the habit of giving that commodity away."

"Stop calling me that."

"It's your name."

"My name is Lina."

"But you are a princess."

"And you are a cold-blooded Neanderthal, but I show you the respect of using your name regardless."

"Fine, *Lina*. Are you ready to go?"

"I need to pack, but I would still like to know where we are going."

His look told her she could go right on wanting answers. He wasn't giving them away. Fine. If that's the way he wanted to play it. She wasn't ready to tip her hand by going all stubborn on him. She could guess their destination anyway. She figured they were headed for the airport in either Reno or Lake Tahoe. Tahoe was closer, but its airport was much smaller. Considering the type of rental car he had, there was a better chance the agency he'd rented from had a drop off at the Reno airport. Not that that sort of thing would be a major hurdle for a man with Sebastian's resources, but business tycoon or not, he was a fan of efficiency.

Okay, so maybe she'd read an article...or ten...about him over the years.

The only thing she couldn't be sure of was whether or not he'd take her directly to the airport or to a hotel. She started packing her things in a Gucci duffel bag her aunt had given her for her last birthday. She hadn't brought much with her when she'd flown the coop and it only took a few minutes to pack her possessions. She shoved the used swimsuit in the outside pocket of the backpack that matched her duffel bag.

She'd laughed when she'd opened them and smiled now at the memory. Her aunt knew her pretty well and managed to give her gifts she would use, even if they were wildly more expensive than anything she would buy for herself. She had far more important things to do with her money.

She slung the backpack over her shoulder and grabbed the duffel bag. "I'm ready to go."

"That's it? No arguments...no demands to tell

you where I'm taking you before we leave the room?" He sounded truly befuddled by her submissive façade.

Good. A confused enemy made an easier enemy to outwit. "Nope. No arguments."

His eyes narrowed, but he didn't say anything further. He took her duffel from her with such a natural movement, she let him have it. There was no reason to hold it back anyway. Everything important was in a money belt concealed under her clothes.

He tossed the duffel in his trunk and she noticed a black case in there as well. So, he wasn't checked into a hotel nearby, not that she'd expected him to be.

They arrived in Reno late that evening. Hawk took Lina to the luxury villa, high in the hills on the outskirts of the city, that his agency had arranged for them. He hadn't apprised King Fahd that his daughter was in custody yet. Hawk was a superstitious soul when it came to his baby, Hawk Investigations, since giving an incorrect report to a client a year ago, he did not report in until he was absolutely sure of his facts. It had been one of his operatives that had taken the pictures of the wrong twin, but that did not mitigate Hawk's sense of responsibility about the false report.

He used the code his PA had texted him on the drive to disarm and open the door. He let Lina into the house and went back to the car for the cases. He doubted she would run in the dark up here in the hills. It was one of the reasons he'd requested this location for their accommodations.

Lina was in the kitchen getting a glass of water when he came back inside.

"I set the house alarm, so don't open any doors or windows."

She rolled her eyes. "You really think that's necessary."

"It pays to be cautious."

"Well, no one would accuse you of being sloppy."

"So…."

She turned to face him, taking a sip of her water. "Yes?"

"No arguments about how I shouldn't be taking you back to your family. No appeals to my democratic beliefs about human rights and liberties?"

A brief flash of anger burned in her doe-brown eyes before it banked and she shrugged. "What would be the point? I learned all I needed to know about how much you respected my privacy and personal rights eight years ago. You showed me then that you would do or say anything to get the job done. I fully expect you to do the same this time around."

While he understood her cynical view of him, it still stung. And it shouldn't. Her opinion of him should not matter at all, but just like eight years ago—she was already becoming more than just an assignment. "I'm not the one letting people down here, Princess."

She frowned. "Neither am I."

"So, the security company that lost your father's account because of your little flit and the guard that lost his job…how do you not see yourself letting them down?" Damn it, what was the matter with him? Maybe Lina wasn't living up to what her family considered her responsibilities, but she wasn't a criminal.

"First, the company having my father's account is not my responsibility, it's theirs. Second, I made sure the security guard was compensated for losing his job," she said, ticking the items off on her fingers. "And if you check, you'll discover he already has a new one with better benefits."

"What do you mean he's been compensated? Did you pay him off to look the other way?"

Her body stiffened with affront. "I did not. I wouldn't compromise someone else's integrity like that. I arranged for payment after the fact."

"Like you supposedly arranged for another job offer?"

"Exactly."

"You expect me to believe that after he lost you, he had no problem getting a better job?"

"It all depends on how you define better. I found out that Rodney didn't really like being a bodyguard, but he didn't think he had any other marketable skills since he got out of the military. I encouraged him to take classes at the local college when he wasn't watching me. When it came time to part ways with him, he was educated enough to qualify for a job he really wanted. With the proper recommendation of course."

"Which you gave him."

"Yes."

"Wow."

Lina's look said she thought he was being sarcastic, but he wasn't. He was really impressed. She'd cared enough about her bodyguard not only to get to know him, but to have a backup plan for when she took a flit. "How long have you been planning to run?"

"Believe it, or not, it wasn't a plan. The timing

just worked out for Rodney to move on the same time I did. I was planning to encourage him to go for the other job anyway."

"Still the social activist, huh?"

"You've read my file, so you know the answer to that."

"Your file says that you work for an environmentalist group and spend your few off hours volunteering at a shelter for runaway teens."

"Technically I no longer work for the organization."

"You can do just as much good in your role as princess, maybe even more." He wanted to believe that. Lina without her causes wouldn't be his princess at all.

"Is that supposed to make me feel better about having my life hijacked?"

"No one is hijacking your life."

"Really? So, my father would be fine with me walking out of here? You wouldn't follow me?"

Unreasonable anger tinged with guilt surged

through him, but he kept his voice even. "You know that's not true."

She simply looked at him as if to say that her point had been made.

"Your father is worried about your safety. Leaving behind your security was not a smart move, Lina." Hell, the truth? Even if he just now realized it, was that half the reason he'd come after her himself was because he'd been worried about her.

She crossed her arms under her breasts, lifting them in purely innocent enticement. "My father's only concern for me is my ability to further his political agenda. As for leaving behind my security detail, I believe we had this discussion once before. If no one knows who I am, then there can be no threat to my safety."

"If you believe that, I've got several thousand police reports where women are victimized for you to read."

"Oh, please. Every other woman lives in the same world as those police reports and ninety-nine-point-nine percent of them don't have bodyguards."

"You are not those women."

"What makes me so different?" she demanded.

"You're a princess. You were raised in a privileged environment."

"And I've spent the last five years living a normal life. I'm no more at risk than any other woman out there."

"That's not true." And her refusal to see that she couldn't hide from who she was did not bode well for her future.

"It's a moot point and this discussion is a waste of both our time. Where am I sleeping?"

According to information from his PA, there were two bedrooms, a fully functioning office and a game room upstairs.

"In one of the bedrooms on the upper floor."

"You're going to let me pick my own room?" she asked in a voice tinged with false surprise and mockery.

Damn it. He was just doing his job. "Yes, you

can pick whichever room you want," he managed to get out between gritted teeth.

He followed her up the stairs, grabbing both her duffel and his bag before she had a chance to. She walked straight into the bedroom on the left at the end of the hall without even giving the other a glance. He followed her and dropped her duffel on the bed.

"Thank you." Her voice was soft and so damn alluring.

He didn't back away when she turned. He couldn't. He wanted to take in her scent, to feel her warmth even if he was determined not to touch her. "You're welcome. Our flight is in the afternoon. We'll be leaving for the airport right after an early lunch."

"Noted." She looked up at him, her dark eyes filled with deep thoughts, but she didn't say anything. Nor did she move away.

"What?"

"I always wondered…"

"What?"

"Was it *all* part of the act?"

His body jolted with shock. Maybe he should have expected that question, but he hadn't. He wanted to explain himself, but just like eight years ago—he wasn't sure what to say. It was the main reason he hadn't pushed harder for a chance to talk.

He didn't pretend not to know what she was talking about, even if it might have been the smarter thing to do. "No."

She bit her lip and nodded, backing away from him. "Thank you. I don't think I want to know which parts."

It was his turn to nod. He'd regretted few things in his life as much as he had his lack of control with Lina. He had been totally disgusted with himself that final night. He couldn't believe he'd allowed himself to get lost in her physical presence again. Once more, his libido had put her at risk and he'd been sick with himself.

His self-disgust had made him harsher with

her than he had meant to be when revealing the truth of his assignment. He'd had eight years to come up with a multitude of different scenarios for the revelations of that night, not one of them leaving his princess looking so damn wounded and betrayed.

She'd moved over to the window and stood looking out at the darkened desert. He didn't know what she could see, but doubted it was the view she was focused on anyway. He walked up behind her and placed his hand on her shoulder.

She shivered and he wanted to pull her body into his, but he had more self-control at thirty-five than he had had at twenty-seven and he didn't do it. "I'm sorry, princess."

"For?" she asked in a voice husky with emotion she was obviously trying to hide.

"I should never have let things get out of hand between us. I compromised your safety twice with my inattentiveness."

She laughed, but the sound was hollow. "You're sorry you didn't do your job right?"

She shook her head as if trying to clear it. "Don't worry about it. As far as I could tell, you did it perfectly."

"I'm also sorry I hurt you." There, he'd said it. And it could go down in the record books because he could count on one hand the number of times he'd apologized in his life and this counted for two of them.

"Is that why you took this job? So you could tell me you were sorry?"

"Yes, partly. I don't do fieldwork any longer."

"You're too busy with your multitude of other business interests."

"It sounds like you've been keeping up with me."

"You know what they say. It's important to know your enemies."

He felt something tighten in his chest. "I'm not your enemy."

"You aren't my friend."

"I was once."

"So you could keep an eye on me. That's not

friendship, that's an overdeveloped sense of responsibility where your job is concerned."

"I liked you, Lina. I respected you."

The harsh sound that came from her throat was all disbelief.

"I did. I still do. You've done a lot with your life, most of it without anyone's encouragement or help."

"That's not true. My aunt and uncle have stood behind me."

"I'm glad there are people in your family you feel you can trust."

She said nothing.

He fought a sigh. This apology thing was so not his gig. "I should have told you the truth about who I was once I realized how hard it would be to keep my hands off you." Try impossible. He forced himself to drop his hand from her shoulder and move back.

She nodded. "Thank you."

He didn't know what to say to that so he said nothing.

"Is that what you wanted to tell me when you called that time?"

"Yes. And when I tried to talk to you the night you learned the truth."

"You had already said a lot."

"Believe it or not, princess, that was a bad night for both of us."

Her shoulders tensed.

"If you respected me so much, why did you accuse me of not caring about the people who depend on me?" She turned to face him, for once her expression open for reading. Skepticism and unhappiness marked her features. "You made the same accusation tonight."

He had and she'd put him firmly in his place. "I made assumptions then and now about your lack of concern. Eight years ago, I thought you knew the effect your actions would have and did not care."

"But I didn't know. It never occurred to me that my bid for personal freedom might cost someone their job."

"Because you were overly confident in your ability not to get caught."

"A wealth of confidence should be something you understand."

He found himself almost smiling at that. "Yes."

"You made the same assumption this time."

"And I was wrong."

"It doesn't matter, though, does it? You still think I owe my father my life and my happiness."

"I thought you believed that line of reasoning was useless to argue with me." But damn it, she was wrong. What he believed was that she had no choice and she would be happier if she made the best of the life she'd been born to.

She seemed to wilt. "It is. I'm tired, Mr. Hawk. Do you mind if I go to bed?"

CHAPTER EIGHT

LINA woke up just before sunrise.

She'd slept surprisingly well considering how disheartened she had been when she went to bed. Sebastian had given her an apology with one hand and snapped away any comfort that might bring her with the other. He might like *some* things about her and even respect her to an extent, but when all was said and done—the man still believed she had no right to an opinion about her own future.

In that way, he was exactly like her father. For a man raised not a part of any country's nobility, he certainly had a medieval view of what it meant to be born a princess.

Well, no matter what her father and his agent

provocateur regarded as truth, she didn't agree with them and she was not going to be forced into marriage to a man she didn't know, obviously didn't love because of the former and had little hope of doing so considering his womanizing reputation.

Actually she'd researched her supposed fiancé pretty thoroughly, almost as intensively as she'd researched Sebastian Hawk over the past eight years, and she thought she and Amir could be friends. They both chose to live modern lives outside the normal sphere of their royal families. He was called the *Playboy Prince*, but he'd never gotten a woman pregnant and refused to stand by her, or had an affair with a married woman, or even broken an engagement.

He dated. A lot. But he also oversaw his family's holdings in the U.S. and did an excellent job with them. He didn't dismiss his responsibilities in favor of play, nor did he ignore the needs of the less fortunate. The Faruq al

Zorha businesses in the States donated more than fifteen percent of their profits each year to worthy causes, and not simply politically expedient or popular ones.

Her impression of him was so favorable that she had considered meeting and getting to know him more than once, but in the end she knew it would be useless. She wanted love in her marriage, or she preferred to remain unattached. If she had children, she was determined to give them a different upbringing than she had had. No matter how much her aunt and uncle had loved her, Lina had never been able to completely dismiss her parents' rejection.

They'd simply given her away. She'd been a thank you to the childless couple for their loyal service to her father, just as if she had been a prize stallion or other possession.

At the age of six, she had not been able to stop her parents from treating her like an object rather than a person, but she was twenty-seven now—an adult fully capable of influencing her own destiny. Her father needed to learn that people were not commodities and if she was the only one willing to teach him that particular lesson, so be it.

She got out of bed and walked quietly to the adjoining bathroom, thinking Sebastian was probably still sleeping and not wanting to wake him. She could use some time to herself this morning to get her thoughts sorted and plan her next move.

She was so focused on her inner reflection that she had stepped inside the bathroom before she realized two things at once. The first, the light was on and she hadn't been the one to flip the switch. And the second, Sebastian stood there naked, preparing to step into the shower.

Her brain short-circuited as her body reacted in a way it hadn't to any stimulus since she was nineteen.

For as intimate as they had gotten when she was in college, she had never seen him naked. She'd never seen any man without his clothes on and it was a revelation. Bronzed skin stretched over sculpted muscle *all over*. Dark silky whorls of hair covered his chest and torso, arrowing down to his manhood. That particular appendage fascinated her and she reached out to touch it without thinking. Her fingertip barely grazed the tip. The skin was surprisingly smooth, like satin. As she watched, the flesh grew rigid, flushing with color.

It was big. Much larger than she had expected. Men and women had been copulating for millennia, so she had to assume the fit wasn't a problem, but she couldn't quite imagine how that would be true. The now hard shaft bobbed under her gaze, curving up toward his taut stomach and Sebastian made a sound halfway between a groan and a sigh.

It was the first sound either of them had made since she walked into the bathroom. Yet the spell of silence surrounding them did not break further.

She was too entranced to even look up at his

face. She wanted to feel more of that satin-smooth flesh. Was it as warm as it looked?

Without realizing she'd done it, she had moved closer so his body was mere inches from her own. She could smell his male musk. Was that what arousal smelled like? It was heady, like a drug. Sucking her bottom lip between her teeth, she gave into the urge to touch and brushed her fingertips over the heated flesh. It was hot and both so very soft and incredibly hard...like pulsing stone under a velvet covering. Her fingers curled of their own volition around him. He was too thick for her fingertips to touch her thumb, but he felt just right in her hand. She still couldn't imagine him fitting inside of her, but the pulsing pleasure between her thighs told her she wanted to try.

A pearly drop of wetness formed on the tip of his penis and her nostrils flared as she took in this new scent. So incredible. She took a deep breath, a tiny moan escaping her throat as her body reacted.

Sebastian pressed his forehead to hers. "You need to stop this, princess." His voice came out a hungry growl that went directly to her core.

"Why?" she asked.

"Because if you don't, I'm going to pick you up and carry you to my bed and I won't be letting you out of it until I've touched and tasted every centimeter of your skin."

That sounded good to her.

He made a pained sound and it was then that she became aware of how tightly wound he was, his entire body rigid with tension. His big hands were curled into tight fists at his sides. A fine tremor shook him and she knew he was fighting what was happening between them with everything in him.

"Please, princess. We can't do this." He sounded so desperate; she could not ignore his plea.

She pressed her hand down his shaft just once before pulling it away. A guttural groan came from deep in his chest. She knew she had to step back from him and return to her own room, but she didn't want to. She wanted to revel in this feeling, to experience an aspect of her femininity that had been missing since his betrayal eight years ago.

She tilted her head back so that their eyes met, then her gaze flicked to his mouth. Would his lips taste the same? Was she sure she remembered that flavor right? Would his kisses affect her the way they had when she was nineteen? She had to believe they would because everything about him brought about an intense response in her.

"Kiss me," she whispered in the air between their lips.

Hawk's lips were eager to do just that, but he knew that even the most chaste kiss would lead to him taking Lina to his bed. He couldn't do that. She was an assignment, not a girlfriend. Technically she was engaged to another man. All of the reasons that had existed eight years ago for not giving in to his urges continued to be valid. She was still a princess. He was still determined not to make a fool of himself over a woman. She was still a nonrunner for a short-term affair. There was still no possibility of a future between them.

Plus one.

It took him several long seconds to work up the strength to gently push her away. Even that touch felt like it burned him; it made him want more. But more was something he was determined *not* to have. "No, sweetheart. We can't." Then he said the one thing that for him was irrefutable. "You belong to another man."

It was as if an ice storm had blown into the room, it got so cold.

Lina's gaze could have frozen lava as she put more distance between them. "Even if I had agreed to marry a man, I wouldn't belong to him like a pet dog. We might conceivably belong to each other in an emotional sense, but my commitment would be just that. A commitment, not a contract of indenture. And in *this* case, I did not agree to marry anyone. I am not engaged and I have made *no* promises of fidelity. If I had, rest assured I would not be in this bathroom with you."

With that, she spun on her heel and left, slamming the door behind her.

Lina was so angry she could spit nails. That arrogant prehistoric *male*! How dare he imply she belonged to Amir? Okay, so, according to Sebastian, she *was* engaged to the sheikh. But she wasn't, darn it. She wasn't! And she wasn't going to be.

But even worse? Was the realization that she was a virgin at twenty-seven and it looked like the only man she wanted…might ever want… to change that was in league with her father to treat her like she was a possession, not a person.

How could this be? She had her theories about why she was…well for lack of a better word, *frigid* and not one of them included the prospect that she was a one-man woman and he was her man. Or at least her chosen physical mate.

The very thought made her stomach churn. The last thing she wanted was to be irrevocably connected to a man who had betrayed her the way Sebastian had done. Moreover, he was so much more like her father than she would ever have believed, even after the debacle when she was nineteen.

No, that couldn't be it.

She'd only tried dating a couple of times in college, both at least a full year after the last time she'd seen Sebastian. The results had been less than auspicious. Her new security measures had resulted in her being outed as a princess and that had subsequently led to her inability to be sure the men wanted her for herself.

After her minor rebellion and the loosening of her security, she'd tried dating again, but even when she was fairly sure she was being dated because the man liked her, there was always a tingle of doubt. What if he had been hired by her father to keep a closer eye on her like Sebastian had been? To this day, she wasn't sure any of her dates had been purely legit.

Which probably said way too much about insecurities she'd rather not face.

But Sebastian's betrayal had destroyed her ability to trust. Both her own judgment and in the honesty of men who expressed interest in her.

She'd always assumed that she needed to be able to trust a man in order to feel the things that Sebastian had brought about in her so many years ago. Well, that theory had been blown to Hades because of all men, she certainly didn't trust *him* now. Yet there was no denying the way he impacted her senses. Or was that her hormones?

It certainly wasn't her heart. That particular organ was off-limits to him. Forever.

So, what did all this mean for her status as a virgin? Did she have no hope of ever having a normal physical relationship with a man?

Prior to Sebastian's reentry into her life, she'd

convinced herself she was fine with being alone…with being sexually innocent. That was before he reawakened her sensual self. She still wasn't entirely sure she could trust that aspect of her nature, but she recognized it was one she missed. No matter what her mother's opinion would be on the subject.

The prospect that a man who had betrayed her held some irrevocable sway over her libido was completely unacceptable.

A man who had the audacity to believe she *belonged* to the man her parents had chosen for her without her input.

The sound of a growl surprised her and she realized it had come from her. He made her *so* angry.

No way was she going to let him hold her sexuality hostage.

So, how did she fix it? She already knew that trying to do something with another man wasn't going to work. At least not while her body was still tuned to respond to Sebastian.

She'd always kind of thought that if she ever fell in love again, not that she really wanted to—the whole pain and betrayal thing had really soured her on the concept—but that she would be as turned on by whoever she loved as she was by Sebastian.

Now, she wondered if her unresolved attraction to Sebastian was actually blocking her from feeling anything physical *or* emotional for another man. Her memories of the pleasure she'd experienced with him were all wrapped up in an uncomfortable shame she'd stuffed deep inside rather than deal with. The first time at the lake, she'd been so wanton in her response that she had not even realized that Bob had come up on them. Even her doctor hadn't seen her completely naked since she was a very tiny child. The thought that Bob had almost seen her breasts exposed had been extremely disconcerting.

In fact, it still was.

Then the night she learned of Sebastian's

betrayal forever linked sensual pleasure with emotional pain and why hadn't she seen that before?

Because she hadn't cared enough to analyze; because she'd been safer avoiding any sort of intimacy in her life. Her parents' rejection had hurt her more deeply than they could possibly understand. Sebastian's had simply confirmed to her battered heart that it was better off lonely than taking a risk on allowing someone else to hurt her the same way.

How ridiculous that she had allowed the very people she did not want influencing her having more sway over her actions and feelings than anyone else.

This had to be changed.

Again, she wondered how to do that. She couldn't do much about the love thing right now since there was no one in her life she was even close to having that kind of attachment to. But her ability to embrace her physical nature was something else.

If she had sex with Sebastian, losing the last vestiges of her innocence and virginity, wouldn't that break through whatever mental barrier had been holding her back since she was nineteen? It had to.

She knew Sebastian wanted her and that made her feel for the first time in a long time. The only question was: how did she get Sebastian to have conjugal relations with her when they were at odds more than anything else?

She could try seducing him, but that hadn't worked the first time around. It had only taken a single phone call to derail her plans as well as what she'd thought was their relationship. Besides, she wasn't super fond of subtle ma-nipulations. She'd much rather be up-front about what she wanted. She refused to play the games of deception that Sebastian now said he was sorry for.

She turned the problem over in her mind until a decent plan began to form.

* * *

Hawk disconnected the call with his assistant and put his computer into standby. It had been three hours since his confrontation with Lina in the bathroom. The house alarm was still on, so he had left her to her own devices while he caught up on work. Staying out of physical proximity was the safest course of action, but breakfast would be delivered soon and he had to disarm the security system to let them in.

That required being in visually confirming distance of Lina's presence. She hadn't acted like she was getting set to run again, but then she was too smart to telegraph her intentions that way.

And after what had happened before his shower, he had to acknowledge that he had no clue what she was thinking.

He would never have expected her to touch him like she had. Unwelcome arousal and pleasure poured through him at the memory. He had never been so close to coming from a single touch in his life. Hell, he'd almost climaxed from the way she was looking at him.

He'd wanted to kiss her so bad; he'd almost given into her soft order. Only a last remnant of sanity had stopped him. But, man, had he pissed her off when he'd said she belonged to the sheikh.

However, her reaction had not shocked him nearly as much as his own. As he'd said the words, they left an acidic burn in his mouth. Her fury was nothing compared to the urge he'd had to hurt someone. Namely Sheikh Amir bin Faruq al Zorha, the man Lina's father had contracted for her to marry.

He should never have taken this job on. Lina had rocked his world right off its axis eight years ago and it was happening all over again. The situation certainly wreaked havoc on one of his most closely held beliefs. That Sebastian Hawk did not have a heart and if he did, it certainly wasn't going to get wrapped up in a woman's wiles.

Hawk knocked on Lina's door, but got no response. He called her name, but that elicited no response, either, so he opened the door, hoping he would not find her in the process of changing. But the room was empty. He didn't find her in the game room, either. Since he'd come from the office, he assumed she must be on the lower level and went downstairs to find her. After searching the ground floor rooms and calling her name twice, his tension level had racked up to dangerous levels. Lina was not a housebreaker; she did not have the technical knowledge to bypass the alarm system. At least her file had said she didn't, but then her file eight years ago had neglected to mention her interest and proficiency in kayaking.

The garage was empty but for his rental car. Where was she?

He opened a door he had assumed the night before belonged to a closet, only to discover that the house had more amenities than he'd realized. Lina was relaxing in a bubbling spa, listening to an MP3 player. Her eyes were closed and she was leaning back, exposing the delectable column of her neck. Her swimsuit clad breasts were mostly hidden by the churning hot water, but he could see enough of the upper swell to make his mouth water for a taste and his libido go zing.

He walked around the circular, recessed hot tub and laid his hand on her shoulder.

Her eyes opened slowly and a smile that could be labeled nothing short of sensuous curved her lips. "Hello, Sebastian."

He gently tugged the speaker bud from her left ear. "Breakfast will be here soon."

"Oh, are we having it delivered?"

"I'm not the cook you are."

That smile flashed across her lips again. "I would be surprised to find out you could cook at all."

"I can keep myself from starving, but that's about it."

"I guess it's a good thing you're a millionaire so many times over, then. You can afford to have all your meals catered."

"I have a housekeeper in New York."

"I'm not surprised."

"I was surprised to discover that you've been living by yourself for the last four years."

"As alone as I could get with a security detail monitoring me 24/7."

"It was a clever setup, actually."

"It was the best I could do to ensure a measure of privacy and maintain the level of security my father's advisors recommended."

"You designed the security plan?"

"Yes. I researched and found the American security company as well."

"I'm impressed." And he was. She'd arranged to have a physical bodyguard watch her whenever she left her apartment, but when she was home she was monitored by less intrusive video surveillance. Her security team maintained an apartment in her building so they were on the spot without actually being in her face.

The setup would not have worked if she had an active social life, but according to her file, she didn't. She dated so rarely that even her father wasn't worried about her getting involved with an inappropriate man. Of course, the king was totally clueless about Hawk's attraction to and for Lina.

Her volunteering was as scheduled as her hours at work. Basically she'd been living as regimented a life as her parents could wish.

"Why are you so against marrying the sheikh?" he blurted out, but wanted the answer enough not to retract the question.

She cocked her brow in question.

"Your life is not exactly a hotbed of different experiences and experimentations. You would have more freedom married to your father's choice."

"Freedom to do what was expected of me. My life may not seem all that exciting to you, but I spend it doing what is important to *me*. I love my job and the time I spend volunteering. It's fulfilling."

"You could do similar things as the sheikh's wife."

"Right. I want to spend my life *doing*, not making politically expedient visits to visible charities so that I am a credit to my husband."

The doorbell rang and Hawk straightened. "That's breakfast. I'll let them in. Meet me in the dining room?"

"Okay. I'll be there in a few minutes."

The sound of her stepping out of the hot tub followed him out of the room. He ached to turn around and see her in the revealing swimsuit, but he knew his willpower was not up to that kind of temptation.

CHAPTER NINE

LINA walked into the dining room wearing a short T-shirt that did nothing to hide either her gorgeous curves or the fact that she still wore her swimsuit. Revealing a slice of honey-colored skin, the hem didn't even reach the top of her bikini bottoms.

"Can we eat outside? I wanted to go out on the deck earlier, but the alarm was on." She smiled winningly at the server setting the food up on the table. "We can move the food ourselves. It looks delicious."

The young man looked at Lina with a besotted expression that irked Hawk. "I don't mind moving it at all. No problem." He started gathering dishes and headed toward the French doors that led outside.

"I didn't say I wanted to eat outside," Hawk said mildly...he thought.

But the server flinched and froze halfway to the door.

Lina just grinned. "Come on, Sebastian, don't be a spoilsport. Even big business tycoons have to take the time to stop and smell the roses sometimes."

He frowned at her. "I'm not overly fond of flowers."

She laughed. Even the server cracked a smirk.

Hawk sighed, giving in. "All right, we'll eat outside."

"Great." Lina spun and headed outside, making it to the door ahead of the server so she could open it for him.

He smiled his thanks, his gaze traveling over Lina's scantily clad body with unmistakable pleasure.

Hawk stifled a growl and followed them.

As expected, the outdoor furniture was immaculate and ready for the server to place the food. Hawk automatically pulled a chair out for Lina and she took it with another smile that only the most conservative would *not* call flirtatious. What the hell was going on?

She'd been furious with him earlier and now she was treating him like she had before he'd revealed his true reason for making her acquaintance eight years ago. Well, not exactly like... she'd grown up and was a lot more overtly flirtatious now.

Confused, he sat down and tried to figure out what had changed with her while he waited for the server to finish putting the food out. The younger man chatted with Lina as he set dishes on the table and poured juice in crystal glasses.

At one point he was bold enough to touch Lina's hip. "Cute ink."

Hawk's hand snapped out and grabbed the younger man's wrist before he even thought. "Don't touch."

Lina frowned and the server put his other

hand up in a placating gesture. "I was just pointing out I liked her tattoo."

Lina had a tattoo? No way. Hawk would have noticed.

He let go of the other man and barked to Lina, "Let me see."

She rolled her eyes and stood up, cocking her right hip as she did so. "See?"

Damn. There it was. Right over her hipbone. A tiny cartoon animal no bigger than a quarter.

"Can I sit down now?" she asked with exaggerated patience.

"Don't on my account," the server said with a laughing leer.

Hawk gave him a stare he reserved for employees on the verge of being fired, but Lina met the other man shamelessly riposte for riposte until he was done putting their food out.

"Thank you," Lina said before Hawk had the chance.

Though he wasn't sure anything but a snarl would come out of his mouth if he opened it.

And right that second, he felt like doing anything *but* expressing gratitude to the guy.

"No problem," the server said. "Just page me when you're finished and I'll come back to clean up."

"Great, will do," Lina said when Hawk remained silent.

The server nodded and left.

"You were awfully snarly with him."

"You're assuming I'm not like this all the time."

"That's true. I only know of you what you chose to project eight years ago and most of that was probably a façade." She sounded pleased by that assumption, rather than angry.

"The only role I played was that of a student. The rest was me."

She looked at him speculatively. "I wonder."

"You think I'm lying."

"I think you are unaware of how much of yourself you kept under wraps when we were together before."

"What do you mean?"

"You're an intense man, Sebastian. You hid that intensity most of the time eight years ago, but it's been on display pretty much nonstop since yesterday."

"If you say so."

"I do."

To change the subject, he asked, "A tattoo?"

Lina shrugged. "It seemed appropriate at the time."

"Why?"

"It's the Road Runner. He should be a victim, prey…right? But he's not. I needed a reminder I wasn't either, that I didn't have to fit the mold made for me, no matter how hard it seemed to live outside of it."

"When did you get it?"

"The month after you left."

For no reason he could fathom, he felt guilty. It was an unfamiliar emotion and even less comfortable one. When unsure of your defense, go on the offense. It worked in business, why not interpersonal relationships? Not that he had a *relationship* with Lina, but even he couldn't deny she was more than a simple client. "Did you have to wear your swimsuit in front of the catering staff?"

"It was only one server and he didn't seem to mind." She started to eat, making a small moan of pleasure as she tasted the crab Benedict.

"Do you enjoy flaunting yourself in front of susceptible men?" He was aware that he sounded like someone's stern father, but couldn't seem to shut up.

Lina just chuckled. "He was pretty susceptible, wasn't he?"

Hawk tensed, his jaw clenching.

She reached out and brushed his forearm. "Relax. I was just kidding. We were both being friendly. That's all."

Even through his suit jacket and shirt, his body reacted with a jolt to her touch. "Friendly plus half dressed equals flirtatious."

"Whatever you say."

He only wished.

She said, "I wanted to go back into the spa after breakfast, so I didn't want to change, but if it bothers you that much, I'll go put something else on."

"It doesn't bother *me*." As the words slipped out, he realized they were a mistake, but he couldn't call them back.

"So, it only bothers you for other men to see me with a little skin showing?"

"It's a hell of a lot more than a little," he growled, digging the hole deeper.

But she just shook her head. "You know what I think?"

"What?"

"You're projecting your own feelings onto him. You're assuming because you want me that he does, too."

"I didn't say I want you…and why wouldn't he?"

Her laugh was free, sweet and too damn sexy for his libido to stay in check. He'd been semihard since tracking her down in the spa and now his slacks fit like a pair of cycling shorts a size too small.

"Oh, you want me. I saw proof of that earlier this morning."

"It's called a morning erection. All men get them."

"Statistically speaking, that's not actually true, but don't try to tell me your reaction this morning wasn't you getting excited."

"Lina!" Her earthy comment shocked him to the core.

"What? You think that just because I haven't dated a lot, I'm hopelessly naïve?"

"According to your file, you're innocent."

Her perfectly shaped brows rose above a mocking brown gaze. "Was our little interlude at the lake or at Jennifer's apartment in that file?"

"Of course not."

"Well, then…"

"You've had increased security since then."

She shrugged. "I won't argue the point."

"Because there isn't one to argue." It was

more important than it should be—read that *not at all*—for her to confirm that she hadn't had a string of clandestine lovers.

"But," she went on without acknowledging his comment, "let me just point out the lack of practical experience, if I *did* lack it, would not stop me from reading up on the subject."

"You've read books about sex?" Okay, maybe he shouldn't be so shocked, but his sweet, innocently sensual Lina reading sex manuals? It was shocking, but more all too arousing a thought.

"Sure. Why not?"

He didn't have an answer, so he didn't attempt one. They ate in silence for several minutes. Lina seemed perfectly at ease, but Hawk kept thinking about all the things she might have read about.

She delicately dabbed at her lips, put her napkin on her plate and pushed it away. "Have you informed my father or his advisors of my location?"

"Why? Are you hoping to convince me to let you go?" He frowned at the thought, for once unsure what he would do if faced with that kind of test to his commitment to his assignment. Nevertheless, he said, "I won't do it. Even after what happened this morning."

"You mean what *almost* happened?" she asked teasingly.

"You touched me."

"And you liked it."

He opened his mouth to speak, but nothing came out.

She laughed. Again. "No denial?"

"You aren't going to convince me to dismiss my promise to your father with sex."

"The thought honestly never crossed my mind."

Thank goodness for small favors.

"The truth is, I'm hoping to strike a bargain."

"I just said—"

"Not for my freedom. Even if you were willing, you don't have the power to offer that.

Not really. You could withdraw your services, but my father would simply hire someone else."

"That's true." And he was glad she realized it. The thought of some other man escorting her back to her family—using means Hawk didn't want to consider—sent black anger through him.

"But you can give me something I want."

"What?"

"To start with, time."

"Lina…" he said warningly.

"Not too much time…just a few days."

"And what do you think you have to bargain with?" Curiosity about what it might be ate at him. Was she going to offer her body in exchange for that time? The prospect was way more appealing than he wanted it to be.

"My compliance."

Her answer stunned him. "I have you. I don't need your compliance."

"Are you sure about that?"

"You will probably call me arrogant, but yes."

Flicking her silky cascade of multicolored hair

over one shoulder, she cocked her head to one side. "How do you intend to get me on the plane?"

"I have a letter from your father giving me permission to use whatever means necessary to insure you do."

Lina blanched, but looked no less confident. "And in Marwan, that letter would carry a lot of weight, but we aren't in my father's country."

"It's your country, too, princess."

"No, it is not." She sounded so sure, not at all like a petulant child rebelling against her parents.

"You can't wish away your place in the world."

"No, but I can and did take legal action to change it."

"What do you mean?"

"I am a U.S. citizen."

"Living in this country, even for most of your life does not make you a citizen."

"No, but applying for citizenship and passing the test does."

An ugly word came out of his mouth.

"If you attempt to take me on a plane, or anywhere else for that matter, by force, you risk being faced with kidnapping charges."

"Your father—"

"Has diplomatic immunity. You don't. And while his word may be law in Marwan, his letter of authority isn't worth the paper it's written on when it applies to a U.S. citizen here in the States."

"You're lying."

"I'm not, but you are welcome to check. I'll even give you my social security number to make it easy for you."

"You don't have an SSN."

"I do. I got it when I became a citizen."

"This is not possible."

"But it is."

"If you are a citizen, why did you come with me yesterday?"

"Because I know I have to face my family."

"Why run in the first place?"

She looked away, an expression he couldn't decipher on her face. "You wouldn't understand."

"Your father knows nothing of your dual citizenship." Heck, Hawk couldn't be absolutely sure that she wasn't bluffing, but something in her eyes told him she wasn't.

"It's not dual. I gave up Marwanian citizenship to become a U.S. citizen."

"Why?" In Marwan, she was a princess. In America, she was just another woman from a wealthy if conservative family.

Not that her action really changed who she was. Lina was still the daughter of a powerful king who expected her to marry the man he'd chosen for her. If she refused, she would cause a break with her royal parent that would most likely be irreparable.

Hawk had always maintained that his mother's disloyalty and lack of maternal love did not bother him, but the truth was, if he could have her in his life without her using him...he would. The absence of any real family since his father's death had caused him more than one brooding moment in the past few years.

"Marwan does not offer dual citizenship. My father's family has always expected absolute loyalty from their people."

"It's your family, too, princess."

She shrugged, her face going neutral.

"I can't believe your father is not aware of your change in citizenship."

"It's not something he would have antici-pated. The security team wasn't watching for it, neither were the paper pushers."

"You flew right under their radar," he said with unquenchable admiration.

"Yes."

"You couldn't have done it with the new security measures."

"No. It was seeking my citizenship that caused me to go looking for ways to circumvent my security team in the first place."

"You had your citizenship when we first met?"

"Yes."

"Why did you do it?"

"I knew one day I would need the leverage." She sighed, frowning with a sadness he hated to see. "I don't expect you to understand. You've made your feelings about my so-called duty clear, but when my parents tossed me away, they lost the right to dictate my life. Not that I'm convinced they had it regardless."

"They didn't toss you away."

"Call it what you like, they sent me to live in America. I chose to become an American."

"So, you said you wanted to bargain with me for your compliance?"

"Yes."

"Besides time, what do you want?"

"You, Sebastian. I want you."

CHAPTER TEN

LINA WOULD HAVE LAUGHED at the expression on Sebastian's face if she wasn't so nervous. She'd done a good job so far of hiding her emotions, but the mask was going to start cracking soon if she wasn't careful.

"What the bloody hell do you mean, *me*?"

"It's quite simple, really," she forced past the dryness in her throat. "I want sex with you… more than once, which is why I want time."

"I'm not a gigolo," he ground out, sounding highly insulted.

"And I'm not offering to pay you to have sex with me."

"You might as well be."

"Don't be such a prude. Whether you want to

admit it, or not, you want me." She took a deep breath and let it out. This was harder than she imagined, and she hadn't thought it was going to be a cakewalk. And she hoped to God she was right. "And I want you. For two normal people in a situation less melodramatic than this one, that would most likely end with them in bed together."

"Are you saying you don't think I'm normal, princess?"

"What, a super wealthy man who runs not only a plethora of businesses, but his own inter-nationally renowned detective agency? Nah, that's as normal as it gets."

He shook his head. "You aren't serious about this."

"Like I'm not really a U.S. citizen?"

The sound that erupted from his throat was pure frustration…of the male variety.

"Look, it's not like I'm really asking for something you don't want to give. Think about it, Sebastian." She stood up. "And while you are at it, why don't you page that cute server so he can come back and clean up?"

She peeled her T-shirt off as she walked away. It didn't hurt to give him a glimpse of what she was offering. Lina had a hard time accepting her own bold actions, but then she'd never shrunk from going after what she wanted.

Right now, she needed freedom.

And it was a type of freedom only he could provide. A sexual liberation that unfortunately, it seemed like only this man could give her.

No matter how much she teased him about the hot server.

The other man had touched her hip and it hadn't affected her as much as the way Sebastian had *looked* at her when she stood up to show him her mini-tattoo.

She'd only been sitting in the bubbling hot tub about five minutes when Sebastian came storming into the room. "What about your sheikh?" he demanded in a cold voice.

"For the last time, he's not my fiancé…not my sheikh…not my anything. What you and my father choose to believe does not in any way alter reality. And in reality I never gave my consent, either implied or otherwise, to my father choosing my future spouse."

"You knew he believed he had the right to do so."

"He also believed he had the right to give me away as if I was nothing more than a possession when I was six years old. I didn't agree with that and I don't agree with this."

"You just want sex?" he asked with bad temper. "You aren't expecting this to become something more?"

"Don't worry, Sebastian. I fell for you eight years ago because I thought you were a different kind of man. Don't concern yourself…I could never fall in love with a man so much like my father, no matter how great the sex is."

"Then why the hell do you want it?"

"My reasons are none of your business. The question is, are you willing?"

He cursed.

"Crudely put, but that's the idea, yes."

He glared at her and darned if that didn't turn her on. Her reaction to this man was just too weird. She wanted him pretty much all the time…no matter what his mood. She'd worry about what that said about her if she didn't know how much she *didn't* react to other men. She figured this was a unique response to this man she would not have to worry about once they parted ways.

But she wanted him out of her system. She wanted to be over him. For real this time. And if it took living out the sensual fantasies he sparked in her overactive imagination, then so be it.

He said something under his breath that she couldn't make out.

"What was that?" she asked.

"I said, I can't believe this."

"Really?"

He looked at her like she'd lost her mind. "Really."

"What's so hard to believe?"

"That you are trying to blackmail me into having sex with you." He spoke slowly, like trying to explain himself to someone who wasn't very bright.

She didn't take offense. Sebastian Hawk was one hundred percent pure alpha male. He was accustomed to being in control of any situation that involved him. With the drop of her bombshell about her citizenship, she'd taken away some of that control and he had to be royally ticked off.

"It's not blackmail. It's a bargain. And frankly, you're getting the better side of the deal. There is nothing that says I have to cooperate with you at all, but I have my reasons for doing so. In exchange I want something that if you were honest with yourself and me, you would admit you want as well."

"You're damn audacious."

"You don't think a princess should be bold?"

"You want the truth?"

"It would be nice, yes."

He looked at her for several silent seconds, making her want to squirm under the scrutiny. However, she maintained her nonchalant air… barely.

Then a half smile tipped one corner of his mouth. "I find your honesty and willingness to go after what you want arousing."

Her gaze flicked to the suit slacks tented below his waist and she felt a blush climb up her neck. "I see."

He laughed shortly. "I guess you do. I'm not sure why this whole situation is so tempting to me."

"Um…because you *do* want me?"

"Perhaps, but there is something about an innocent being so brazen that is very exciting to a man like me."

"You are so sure I am innocent?"

"You talk a good game, princess, but you

blushed when you looked at my erection and that says more about your lack of experience than all the bold statements you might make."

She bit her lip, the betraying blush once again heating her skin. "I suppose it doesn't hurt to tell you."

He cocked his head to one side as if waiting for her admission.

"I am still a virgin." There was no reason to spell out just how inexperienced she was. He didn't need to know that no other man had ever touched her as intimately as he had eight years ago.

He nodded.

She sighed.

He laughed again. "Trust me, that is something you want me to know."

"Why?"

"You mean after reading all your books on sex, you don't know?"

"You'll be more careful?"

"I would have anyway, on the chance…but yes."

She'd guessed that…which could have been a dumb assumption to make, but at least now he knew. "So, we have a deal?"

"That depends."

Her heart stuttered in her chest. Was he agreeing? "On what?" she asked with an embarrassing squeak.

He took off his suit jacket. It was slate-gray, obviously an English designer…and why she was noticing that, she didn't know. Maybe because if she focused on the fact he was undressing…that was what he was doing, right? Well, if she focused on that, she might hyperventilate.

He loosened his tie and she bit her lip, wanting very much to ask him what he was doing, but afraid of the answer. What if she was assuming things again and his intent was just to get more comfortable. The spa room was warm after all.

"Lina?"

"Yes?" There went that revealing squeak again.

He unbuttoned the top button on his crisp white shirt. "What exactly are the terms of this deal?"

"Um…terms?"

"Yes, Lina, terms. I'm a businessman. I want to know exactly what you expect in return for your cooperation."

"I already told you." Was he really going to force her to spell it out?

"You want sex. I got that, but you also said you wanted time. How much time are we talking about?"

She swallowed, trying to wet her suddenly parched throat. "I hadn't really considered." Which was the truth, she just knew that one night wasn't enough. But as she admitted that, she felt silly. She was the one who had offered the bargain in the first place, she should have figured out the terms to begin with.

She just knew this was going to put her at a disadvantage.

"I think understandably, I'm not comfortable with an open-ended arrangement. Your father is expecting results." And he knew he couldn't give her anymore.

"And you're not about to have your professional reputation besmirched." Just like eight years ago.

"I would prefer not to, no."

"Um…" She licked her lips. "A week… seven days."

"That's too long. Your father knows I expected to find you before then."

"Just because you expect something to happen, doesn't mean it will."

"It does for me."

"So, this time you can be disappointed."

"I did find you, princess."

"My father doesn't need to know that."

"I have a responsibility to him—he's my client."

"Yes, your responsibility is to make sure that you find and deliver his daughter to him. You can't do that if I refuse to comply…not without facing serious legal charges. So, technically this week *is* what is necessary to fulfill your obligation."

"Three days, princess."

Whether it was the final tenuous link to her belief in romance, or simply her nerve to keep haggling, something broke inside her. Along with the break came anger. She was tired of his denial of a need that anywhere matched her own, but she was past the point of being willing to argue about it any longer. "Fine," she said with cold precision. "If you think we can burn the fire out between us in two nights, then I bow to your superior experience in this area."

His eyes widened. "I expected a counteroffer, princess."

"Then you miscalculated."

"I see that."

She climbed out of the hot tub and walked over to her towel on the bench. Drying off, she ignored him.

"I said three days, not two nights, Lina."

She didn't bother to look at him as she shrugged. "Same thing."

"No, technically, it is not. Three days constitutes the same number of twenty-four hour periods. Starting now, that would constitute three nights as well."

Something lightened inside her that he was maximizing the amount of time they had together, but she didn't allow herself to get all warm and fuzzy. After all, *he* was the one who had argued against a week.

"Duly noted," was all she said as she grabbed her T-shirt from earlier and slipped it on.

"Where are you going?"

"To take a shower."

"We can start there, but I would prefer to spend some time together in the spa."

She looked up then, to discover that he had removed everything but his slacks and the fly was open on them, revealing black silk boxers tented over his hardness. He should have looked vulnerable like that, only half-dressed and asking her if she wanted to go back in the hot tub with him. But he didn't. He looked as commanding as always.

And really, he hadn't asked about the spa, had he? He'd simply stated what he wanted.

"Is that a request, or an order?"

"What do you want it to be?"

Her heart started trip-hammering. "I…"

He moved until he was standing right in front of her and cupped her cheek. "Do you want me to take charge, princess?"

"Is that what your sex partners usually ask for?" she inquired breathlessly.

"There is no room for what others do or do not like here, Lina." His hand trailed down her neck and rested on the side of her breast, not moving, but his thumb a hairsbreadth from touching her nipple.

"I want…"

"Yes, baby, what do you want?"

"I like the hot tub."

He smiled. "That's good, but that's not what I asked."

She swallowed, feeling nervous and yet conversely powerful. He'd asked what she wanted, hadn't tried to convince her one way or another. Despite everything, something inside her craved the chance to trust in this man. "What I choose…does it last the whole three days?"

"Let's just make it for the time while we're in this room."

"Okay."

"Okay, what?"

"I want you to take charge." Her heart was nervous…her mind wasn't so sure…but her body knew with a primal instinct she could not dismiss that they both needed this.

The tiny flicker of relief in his gray eyes confirmed it.

His thumb covered the tiny distance to make contact with her nipple. Despite the two layers of cloth between her skin and his, she felt the touch like an electric jolt that reached not only that one spot, but her other breast tingled as well and she felt an intense pulse of pleasure between her legs.

"Are you sure, princess?" And something in

his expression said he was asking about more than him being in control.

She sucked her lower lip between her teeth and looked deeply into his eyes. Along with that subtle message, all she saw was desire, pure and honest sexual need. "You won't try to deny your sexual need for me anymore?"

"No."

"Or hide behind a man who has no claim on my life?"

"No." This was practically growled and the flash of anger that darkened his features surprised her.

So, Sebastian didn't like the idea of her with her father's chosen, either.

"For three days…seventy-two hours…there is only room for you and me." Which was a far cry from acknowledging that she had no obligation where Amir was concerned, but it was better than nothing.

On some level Sebastian had to realize the sheikh had no legitimate claim on her. If he hadn't, Sebastian would not be touching her right now. His sense of personal honor was too great, no matter how strong his sexual interest in her.

She would have to be content with reading the message into some things that simply were not going to be said.

"Then, I am sure."

His lips tilted in one of his rare smiles. "Good."

She appreciated the fact that he had not asked her if she was certain she wanted him to be her first lover. Again, his actions spoke more eloquently than his words. His lack of belaboring the point of her virginity told her that he respected her enough to accept that she knew her own mind.

She would not deny that a small part of her wished this was happening on her wedding night, but she accepted that if she could not get over Sebastian, chances were she would never have one of those. She certainly had no intention of sharing such a thing with Sheikh Amir.

Sebastian leaned down to kiss her. It was barely a brush of lips, but it somehow sealed their deal. Both the three days and her assertion she wanted him to take charge right now.

He grasped the hem of her T-shirt. "I'm going to take this off."

She nodded, raising her arms so that he could remove it easily.

She had worn a swimsuit in front of him on several occasions, but she felt more exposed as her top got dropped to the floor and the suit was revealed this time.

His gaze traveled over her, making contact like a touch and she trembled. "You are so beautiful."

"Am I?" It was not something she thought of herself.

"Yes." He reached out to trail his fingertips from her temples down her body until he reached her hips. Then he stopped. "You are the most alluring woman I have ever met or seen."

The praise was over the top, but she had no

doubts of his sincerity. Sebastian was not the type of man given to empty flattery.

Her tummy fluttered. "I'm glad you see me that way."

"And I'm glad you want me anything near like I want you."

Finally he had admitted it out loud. She had no idea how much she'd needed to hear the words until they came out of his mouth and her knees gave way in relief.

His hold on her hips tightened and he pulled her closer to him. "You okay, princess?"

"More than," she admitted, feeling his honesty deserved her own.

"I'm going to kiss you then I'm going to take off your swimsuit top. And I'm going to look at you like I wanted to do eight years ago."

"Yes," she said on a breath of sound.

He made good on his words, closing the distance between their mouths with slow inevitability that had her entire body straining for the kiss by the time their lips met. Her body melted into his as she tasted the flavor that had haunted her dreams for too long. His tongue dipped into her mouth and then retreated. She whimpered a protest, but he just nipped at her lower lip.

"Sebastian."

"Be patient, for me. I'm going to make this so good for you, but I need you to cooperate." He didn't give her a chance to respond, but renewed their lip-lock.

It was so good. His lips molded hers, moving and sending waves of pleasure through her. Needing an anchor in the swirling fog of her senses, she reached up to grab his shoulders and touched hot, silky *naked* skin over rigid, bulging muscle. Her eyes flew open to find his had never closed. He was staring down at her with dark, piercing ardor.

She moved her hands down his chest, asking with her gaze if it was all right to touch. His answer was another flick of his tongue against her lips. She took that as approval and she explored the hair roughened contours of his chest.

So strong…so hot…he was such a perfect example of masculine power. Her fingertips slid over his nipples. They were hard. She'd read that for most men, they were erogenous zones. She played a little, circling, lightly scraping her nails over the pointed nubs.

He groaned and stepped back, grabbing her wrists so she could no longer touch him.

She looked at him questioningly.

"You know what comes next."

She remembered what he'd said and her heart fluttered. "Yes," she whispered.

He smiled, approval shining in his gunmetal gaze.

She took a deep breath and let it out as he released her wrists. Then, he reached behind her to unhook first the bottom, then the top strap of her bikini top. It fell away from her body, dropping to the floor and making a small wet plop as it landed. Neither of them looked down to see, though.

Her eyes were glued to his and his look was set on her newly revealed flesh with tactile strength.

"How do you do that?" she asked, perplexed.

"What?"

"Touch me with your eyes."

He shook his head. "I don't know. I only know that watching you is like a feast for my senses."

"Don't you want to touch?" she dared to ask.

"Oh, I definitely plan on touching you, princess, but right now I want to look."

"That's all?" she asked, her voice catching.

"For the moment."

She said nothing, did not know what she should say if she did speak. She had told him he could be in control and the truth was, it was exciting her beyond anything she would have believed possible to have relinquished the power of decision-making to him. She really did need this.

Her body kept telling her that no matter what

had happened with him in the past, or what might happen in the future, she could trust him. It wasn't logical, but at present, she didn't care a penny for logic.

She just wanted to keep feeling what she was experiencing right this moment in time.

She did not know how long she stood under his burning surveillance. Time became elastic, seconds could have been minutes and vice versa. Nothing existed for her but his eyes on her. Her gaze flicked over him, noting the changes watching her elicited in him.

His jaw hardened as if he was biting back words and his body tensed, the bulge in front of him unbelievably growing. A wet spot formed on the black silk of his boxers where the tip of his manhood pressed against the fabric.

She'd read about pre-ejaculate…she'd seen it that morning, but knowing that merely studying her visually was causing it now, gave her a strong sense of feminine sensual power.

She'd given him control, but that was precisely the point. She'd *given* it to him and her willingness to trust in him, to his perusal, was inflaming him. That knowledge felt almost as good as his kisses.

"I want to see all of you before I start touching you," he said in a guttural voice.

CHAPTER ELEVEN

LINA licked her lips nervously and took a breath before speaking. "Okay."

"Take off your bottoms."

"Me?"

"You."

"But—"

"If I do it, I'll touch you and I'm not ready to do that yet."

"You look ready to me."

He laughed, releasing a measure of the tension building between them. "Too ready. Now, do as you're told, princess."

"Maybe I shouldn't. I don't think princesses are supposed to take orders."

"You are *my* princess…for now…that means you can take my orders."

"If I want to."

"I thought we established that you did."

She smiled, letting her actions speak for her as she went to push her bikini bottoms down her hips. Considering her background, she should have felt self-conscious baring herself to him, but she didn't. All she felt was an eagerness to witness his reaction to seeing her as no one else had in her adult life.

She was not disappointed. A sound came from deep in his chest somewhere between a growl and a moan. His eyes narrowed, but his pupils dilated with arousal and his already tense body went rigid as if he was physically having to hold himself back from touching her.

She shook under his scrutiny, moisture making itself known between her thighs. Aching with sensation even though they were not being touched, her nipples tightened so that she could feel their pebble hardness in the softly circulating air of the room. In the end, it wasn't him that moved, but her, her feet taking her closer to him of their own volition.

"Stop."

"I can't," she said as she took another step.

With a sound that was torn from his throat, he reached out the remaining gap between them and grabbed her shoulders, then pulled her toward him with barely leashed savagery. His mouth slammed down onto hers with erotic force, his tongue taking instant possession of her interior. Her tongue battled for supremacy with his while her lips moved against his in instinctive pleasure that was in no way limited by her lack of experience.

Okay, so maybe she'd practiced a time…or twenty… on her hand, but still…it felt so right and man, was it good. He didn't seem to mind her aggression, either. In fact, if the way he grew progressively more uncontrolled was any indication, he liked it a lot.

She liked it, too, but she *loved* the way it felt

when her bare breasts rubbed against his chest. It was the most amazing sensation and her lips actually went slack as she concentrated on enjoying it. Sebastian didn't stop kissing her, though, forcing her lips to mold to his even though she wasn't consciously doing so.

She was focused on moving in small increments. Side to side. Up on her tiptoes and down again. Back just a little bit and then forward until she was pressed firmly against him. All of it felt brilliant. So, she did it again. All of it. His lips owning hers while she used his body to explore new sensations with her own.

Had she really reached the age of twenty-seven without ever feeling this before?

How?

But the answer was more disturbing than satisfying. No other man in her life had been him. Which was why she was doing this, she reminded herself. So, enjoy it, already. Right.

She found that she liked it best when her nipples barely brushed over his when she was going side to side, so she did that several times until the emptiness growing in her womb grew so acute she cried out in inarticulate need against his marauding mouth.

He seemed to understand, though, because he pulled his lips from hers and brushed them over her forehead, then her cheeks. "Shh…princess, it's all right. I'll take care of you."

"I need something, Sebastian. Please."

"I know what you need."

"Yes."

"Do you trust me?"

Instinct answered over her brain's automatic negative. "Yes."

And that word felt far too right.

"Then just stand there. Let me bring you down a little."

"I don't want to come down," she whined. Oh, gosh…when was the last time she had whined? It was not her. But then neither was this needy wanton.

"Yes, you do."

She looked at him and read his sincerity in a gray gaze gone almost black with his own need. She took a deep breath and let it out slowly. "Okay."

He nodded.

She smiled despite her unfamiliar but acute sensual hunger.

He stepped back…only a few inches, but enough to break body contact. He cupped her face and looked into her eyes. "Just breathe for me, princess."

It was then that she realized she was panting in short shallow breaths and she had to concentrate on breathing in and breathing out. The severe, almost painful arousal coursing through her began to scale back slightly.

It wasn't like she lost her desire, but she became aware of the whir of the overhead fans, where before all she could hear was his inhalations and exhalations. The sound of the hot tub jets running as it maintained temperature encroached on her consciousness.

She looked around her, seeing the opulent room with new eyes. The recessed spa bubbled gently in one corner and the smooth as glass water of the indoor-outdoor pool glistened in the other. Now that the outer doors had been opened, she'd been able to open the divider that made the pool accessible to the outside and she could even hear the fall of the oversize fountain in the center of the outdoor portion.

"If you want me to cool down a little, maybe we should go in the pool rather than the spa," she said.

Sebastian's smile was so sexy, it undid the last few seconds of her calming down process. "Good idea, beautiful."

"So, you're going to take off your pants?" she asked with undisguised interest.

"After you get in the water."

She pouted.

He laughed. "Do you have any idea how adorable you are when you do that?"

She shook her head. She never pouted, so how

could she? Did he really think she was adorable? But his continued smile said he did indeed. Wow.

"So, you want me to get in the water?"

"Yes."

"And you *are* going to join me, right?" She had no desire to "cool down" alone.

"Of course, princess. What would be the fun otherwise?"

"Okay then." She turned and walked to the steps that led down into the water. Though she knew it was heated and had dunked her hand in it earlier to test the temperature, finding it perfect, it now felt chilly against her overheated skin.

She forced herself to descend into the pool until the sound of fabric sliding against skin arrested her. She spun to face him, barely keeping her balance on the bottom step. Sure enough, his pants were already in a puddle of expensive fabric on the floor of the room. He pushed his boxers down past his hard-on and it bobbed up toward his belly. Was it bigger than it had been that morning?

She gulped. It certainly looked like it.

He started walking toward her and she nearly choked on her own breath. Still, his body was amazing. In motion, it was a work of art. A masterpiece at that.

"You're watching me like you want to devour me."

"Maybe I do."

His body jerked and he stopped. "Don't say things like that with that beautiful as sin mouth. You are going to give me ideas you are not ready for."

And it was then that she realized how her words could be taken. Oh. "Who says I'm not ready? You think I don't want that?"

He groaned. "Please, princess…be quiet, for just a minute."

She shrugged in acquiescence, but then turned and dove into the water, swimming to the end of the indoor section of the pool. It wasn't very long, but it was long enough…to give him a glimpse of her body in motion. If it affected him like it had affected her to see him then her silence wasn't going to have the impact on his escalating libido that he wanted.

Some part of her insisted she push his limits. She was aching to consummate their relationship…uh…*deal*. It was a deal, not a relationship and she so had to remember that, but the internal reminder sent a pang of pain through her heart.

Strong hands grasped her around the waist and she went swishing backward through the water until her body landed against his. "There are consequences for teasing a hawk."

"Are there?" she gasped out.

"Yes."

"What are they?"

"Hawks are predators, what does that make someone they catch?"

"Prey?" she asked in a whisper.

"Exactly."

"I think I want to be your prey, darling Sebastian."

His body shuddered. "Say that again."

"That I want to be your prey?"

"What you called me."

"Sebastian?" she teased.

He just growled into her ear and she shivered. Then she went still. "Darling."

"I like that." He sounded confused and not a little bothered by that fact.

She laid her head back on his shoulder. "I do, too."

He turned her to face him. "I have never wanted another woman as much as I want you."

Again he sounded bothered and she did not comment on the surprising admission. Or at least she did not plan to, but words just sort of came out of her mouth. "If only you had wanted me that much eight years ago."

Then none of this would be necessary.

If a tiny voice deep in her mind questioned that assertion, she chose to ignore it.

"I did."

She shook her head. "No. You walked away."

"You didn't have anything to blackmail me with back then. Well, you did, but you didn't realize it."

Her head spun…was he only touching her because of the deal? That's what he'd said. He'd also said she could have attempted blackmail eight years ago.

Then she realized with perfect clarity what he was talking about. Eight years ago, she'd been so devastated by his betrayal, she had not even considered that he had betrayed her father as well. Or at least his own work ethic by touching her as intimately as he had.

It had been a couple of years before she'd been able to analyze the situation with enough distance to give Jennifer's earliest comments on the situation any credence. From the first time Lina had poured her broken heart out all over her friend, Jennifer had insisted that the whole thing could not have been merely a job to Sebastian. Because a man like him would never compromise a sexual innocent in order to do his job, especially if that job involved protecting her.

That realization had healed a tiny portion of the hurt that had shattered Lina's heart and self-confidence. Not enough to make her open to trusting another man, but some.

She scrutinized Sebastian's face, trying to read his expression, trying to understand the coldness creeping through *her* as his words forced another moment of clarity.

She could not decipher his expression, though—or at least make herself believe what she needed to about what he was feeling. He wanted her, a lot. According to him. And well, she believed it because his physical reactions had been blatant. But also, according to him, he would not be acting on that desire without her bargain. Which she had known and yet something inside her had refused to really *know* it, or maybe to accept it as truth.

She'd convinced herself that despite his words, this thing between them was bigger than both of them, not just her. Only now, for whatever reason, his words were sinking into her brain in a way that they had not before. Maybe because he was saying the same thing despite what they had done and the massive evidence of his arousal.

Maybe because he was finally admitting his desire for her in words and yet still denying that he would have acted on it without being forced. Perhaps because he was finally speaking the truth she had been able to discern all along, she felt compelled to believe him about *everything*.

She couldn't hide from the ugly truth. She couldn't live with it, either.

No matter what she'd thought she was ready for. No matter what kind of compromise to her principles she'd thought she could tolerate. Regardless of what she'd thought she wanted, she knew in that instant that she did not want Sebastian as the result of a deal.

She might never get over him, but if she couldn't have him because he truly wanted her…then she could not have him at all.

She pushed away from him and because he was not expecting it, she slipped easily from his arms. She propelled herself backward until she was to the steps.

She stopped with her hand on the rail. "This was a mistake. We can fly out this afternoon as planned. I'll go to D.C. and meet with my father."

Shards of pain were cutting into her, but she refused to go down emotionally like she had eight years ago. At least this time, Sebastian had not lied to her. She had lied to herself.

And, ultimately, isn't that what had happened when she was nineteen? She'd believed he felt the same emotions she was experiencing, not because he'd said he did, but because she had wanted to. He'd betrayed her friendship, but he hadn't betrayed her love. She'd done that all on her own.

And she wasn't going there again. Not for freedom from her sexual repression. Not for *anything*.

"What the hell are you talking about?" Sebastian demanded. "And where the hell are you going?"

"Back to my room…to get dressed and pack."

"What?" he practically shouted. "Why?"

"I don't want to blackmail you into having sex."

"That's not what you were saying a few minutes ago."

"I…" Could she explain and get out of there without losing it? She had to try. Her pride wouldn't allow otherwise. "I thought you wanted me."

"I do want you, damn it."

"Have you noticed you swear a lot when you get upset?"

"What the bloody difference does that make?"

"Um…none. Just noticing, that's all."

"Don't try to change the subject. You promised me heaven and now you are backing away, ready to leave me in hell. Are you scared, princess? I told you I wouldn't hurt you."

"No. It's not that." She still wanted him. Her body was literally aching to return to his arms.

"Then what is it?" His eyes narrowed dangerously. "Is this payback for eight years ago?"

"No! Of course, not."

"Then why are you over there and I am over here?" His body tensed for movement. "To hell with that." Then he exploded into action.

She'd only taken a single step backward before he was *there*, grabbing her waist in a firm grip.

He pulled her toward him and deeper water once again, only stopping once they were on the verge of going outside. "Now, explain. Use small words and short sentences so there's no possibility I'll misunderstand."

Oh, wow…he was really mad, angrier than she'd ever seen him. And yet his hold on her was not bruising and she felt no fear for her person at all.

"I'll go to D.C.…you don't have to have sex with me to gain my cooperation."

"And if I want to make love to you regardless?"

"But you don't. You just said you're only touching me because I blackmailed you into it."

"I also said I wanted you more than I've ever wanted another woman."

"But you wanted me that way eight years ago. You didn't touch me then because I didn't force you into it."

"Lina!"

"*What?* That's what you said."

"I know what I said."

"So, um…you can let me go." She didn't say please, but she wanted to. She needed to get away from him before she begged him to make love to her anyway.

And ended up hating herself.

His head lowered until their foreheads touched and he sighed, a long drawn out sound that caused a pang in her heart. "No, baby, I can't."

"You can't let me go?"

"No."

"Why not?"

"Because I need to make love to you."

"But you said—"

"I know what I said," he interrupted. "I was strong enough to walk away eight years ago without finishing what we started. I might have been strong enough this time without your deal, but then again, maybe I wouldn't have been. I do know that we've gone too far to turn back now...unless you really don't want this."

She pulled her head back so she could look into his eyes. "So, this isn't about the deal. You want me? Even though you know I'll return to D.C. with you regardless."

"Yes."

"And you don't begrudge me three days?"

"I wouldn't begrudge a whole week, but I think we're safer sticking with our original plan."

She didn't ask what he meant by safer. She thought she already knew. And she agreed. She had an awful suspicion that the time they spent together would lead to craving more and more and more. And the longer it lasted, the stronger the craving would get.

If he was being brutally honest, she could, too, if only to herself. And she could admit that this wasn't only about getting over a sexual fixation that might very well afflict her for the rest of her life. It was about sharing something she would never have the chance to experience again with the one man who had ever gotten deep enough into her heart to matter.

She might fall in love again one day, but she knew it would never be like it was with Sebastian. Their connection was something special and no matter what he felt, or didn't feel, she could acknowledge that—inside herself at least—where the admission was safe.

"So, three days."

"Three days."

Then he kissed her and the watershed of emotions she'd just gone through fed the passion he'd sparked earlier until her insides felt like a raging inferno of unsatisfied longing.

The slip-slide of their naked bodies together in the water was amazing. She undulated against him, learning a whole new series of pleasure points. His hands were all over her, mapping her skin, branding her with his touch.

She didn't realize they'd been moving until she felt the cool water of the waterfall showering her skin. They were outside. She tried to make herself care, but she couldn't. This felt right…natural.

The knowledge in the back of her mind that there was an eight foot tall brick privacy wall all the way around the backyard helped. So did the fact that the closest neighbor was at least a quarter of a mile away. She was going to assume the caterer had either already come and gone, or Sebastian had not paged him to return yet.

She had no doubt that her three-day lover was too possessive to allow another man the possibility of seeing her naked. He'd been much too disturbed by the server seeing her in her swimsuit with a T-shirt over it.

So, she relaxed…mentally anyway…and let herself wallow in the feelings he was causing. Her body screamed with pleasure and need. And this time even a dunk in a mountain fed stream wouldn't cool her off.

He swam with her, their lips still locked together, until they reached the steps in the outer pool. Then he swept her into his arms and carried her out of the water.

She broke the kiss to ask, "Where are we going?"

He nodded toward a decadent wrought-iron double lounger under a Roman canopy in the middle of the emerald green grass.

"Oh," she breathed.

He smiled, the look indulgent and warm. She was careful not to read anything more into it than masculine desire. She wasn't going to lie to herself again.

He laid her carefully onto the overstuffed oyster shell cushion and then joined her, covering her body with his.

"Have I told you how beautiful and down-right sexy you are, princess?"

"You might have mentioned it." Her voice was croaky and filled with want.

He kissed his way down to her breast. "It deserves more than a mention."

"Thank you. You're the sexiest man I have ever known."

"Glad to hear it." Then his mouth curved around her distended nipple.

He laved, then sucked, then circled the sensitive peak with his tongue before doing it all over again while his hands were busy touching her all over.

She reached for him, but he grabbed her hands and placed them over the ornate white iron bar at her head. "Keep them there, princess."

"But I want to touch you."

"You agreed to let me call the shots."

"In the room. We're outside now."

"I want you to hold onto the bar. Will you do that for me?"

She couldn't deny him, realized she didn't even want to. "Yes."

If she'd thought his touching before was intense, it was nothing like what she experienced now. He caressed, traced, licked, nibbled and teased every inch of her skin until she was a quivering mass of nerve endings ready to explode.

Then he spread her legs with gentle hands and leaned forward to touch his tongue to the most intimate part of her.

She screamed and came and shook as her body immediately began the climb toward another climax. As he lashed her pleasure spot with his tongue, his finger explored her inner recesses. She felt a pressure...some pain...but it only heightened her pleasure high. Then a second finger joined the first and he pressed them deeply inside, gently massaging a barrier she knew denoted her virgin status.

As she went supernova the second time in

less than a minute, he pressed forward and a sharp pain mixed with her euphoric pleasure.

When he withdrew his fingers, they had blood on them. She saw it through the haze of her satiation and she knew what it meant. He had broken her barrier…claimed her in a way no other man would ever be able to.

A primitive part of her she had not even known existed was fiercely glad.

He surged up until his body covered hers. He pressed his hard penis against her tender flesh, but did not attempt to breach her opening. Instead he thrust against her, his length sliding along her clitoris from root to tip with each pelvic movement.

"What…? I…this…" She couldn't string a coherent thought together, but she knew this wasn't what was supposed to happen.

Only it felt so good and he seemed to be enjoying it as well. His face was contorted in ecstasy as his thrusts increased in speed and pressure. Her body had been so starved for this that she found herself careening toward another climax.

When it came, she heard him shout and felt warm wetness against her belly.

Everything was so intense, she felt like she might pass out, but she clung to consciousness, not wanting to miss a moment of the pleasure.

Sebastian said something against her temple that she could not make out.

"What?" she asked in pleasure slurred tones.

For one second he looked totally freaked out before his usual game face slipped back into place and he shook his head. "Nothing."

"If you say so."

"I want to do this again."

"It's a good thing we have three days."

Something dark crossed his countenance, but he nodded. "Yes."

CHAPTER TWELVE

HAWK tracked Lina down in the living room. She was curled up on the oversize suede leather sofa dozing. He'd left her alone to answer some e-mails and make a few phone calls, but he'd ended up closing down his computer before the in-box was empty and ignoring an important call from Japan in order to find out what she was doing.

It was an addiction.

Not just making love, but simply being in her company.

He enjoyed it. Too much.

For the first time in his life, he considered the possibility that he was in love. With a woman promised to another man. How lacking in intelligence was that?

Only Lina didn't consider herself engaged and because she didn't, he didn't, either. On the first day they were here, she'd said he was like her father. Maybe he was. *In some ways*, but not all ways and certainly not to the point that he was willing to force his princess into a marriage she didn't want.

He'd been a fool to think he could do so from the beginning. No matter what he'd said to her, he realized now that deep in his heart he had agreed to come after Lina himself so that he could once again protect her. This time from her family if need be. How could he have been so unaware of his own motives not to have seen it? Okay, so he was a very stubborn man and he had stubbornly insisted that he was never going to fall prey to love.

Only he had.

And the hell of it was, he didn't even mind.

If only he could believe Lina's family, or even she herself, would respond to his feelings with as much acceptance. She'd said she could never love him because of his similarities to her father, but he was hoping to change her mind. It didn't help that she still referred to their love-making as sex, holding a part of herself back from him. He felt it and it made him crazy, which led him to try to break down the barrier. The only way he knew to do so was to make love.

Again.

Not that they'd actually had intercourse, but they'd done pretty much everything else. He'd told her he wanted to wait until she had healed a little inside before attempting to penetrate her. He didn't want her first time with their bodies completely joined marred by soreness from her broken hymen.

And he was determined to make it their first time, not their last. It was going to happen tonight, their final agreed upon night together.

But right now, he just wanted to be with her. Sappy? Maybe. But true. And he was a big enough man…finally…to admit it. Okay, it also helped to know she was a U.S. citizen. What had been flat out impossible in his mind eight years ago, not shown with the light of hope to his rapidly changing heart.

If her father did not have legal control over her, it was just possible Lina and Hawk could have a future.

He sat down near her feet and her eyes fluttered open.

She smiled…a wide-open expression filled with love, he was sure of it. Then her look shuttered and her welcome turned down a couple of notches.

He stifled his sigh of frustration. This was his fault and he was going to fix it. He'd made a mistake eight years ago when he'd walked away and he'd made a mistake four days ago when he came after her with the intent of taking her back to her family.

He planned to rectify both mistakes in an unmistakable way.

"You said I wouldn't understand why you ran,

even though you knew you didn't have to. I'd really like you to explain it to me now."

"Why?" she asked, her voice still husky with sleep.

He reached out and brushed his fingers through her long hair. "Because I want to know you better…to understand everything about you."

She laughed. "Women aren't that easy to understand, don't you know that? That would take a lifetime."

"Maybe. Would that be so bad?"

Her soft brown eyes widened, but then she shook her head. "You're joking."

It was his turn to say, "If you say so." One of her favorite phrases that he'd figured out pretty quickly meant she wasn't going to argue, but didn't necessarily agree.

She frowned.

He smoothed the line between her eyebrows with his fingertip. "Tell me why you ran."

"I was scared."

"Why? You're a U.S. citizen."

"And my father is a king. I was afraid of what he might do to try to force me to his will…I was afraid of what I might do in some final ditch effort to gain his approval."

"So, you ran in order to shore up your reserves."

"And to force him to send someone else after me, someone who hopefully wouldn't have diplomatic immunity."

Clever. And effective. "Your plan worked."

"In unexpected ways."

"Was it really so unexpected? You had to know he wouldn't use the security company who had lost track of you to begin with."

She sat up, staying close, letting their bodies touch as she settled into her favorite seat in the corner of the couch. "You're right. I think I may have even subconsciously expected him to contact you. After all, it had worked before."

"But you were still disconcerted by my arrival." Not that she'd shown it overtly, but he'd figured it out eventually.

"I think you will always disconcert me, Sebastian."

"And you will always drive me to distraction."

She grinned. "Is this where the kissing starts?"

"Actually it's where I remind you that we are going out tonight and you need to get dressed."

"We went out last night." She chewed on her bottom lip, something she did when she was thinking, or trying to get her courage to the sticking point. "I would rather stay here with you than go anywhere."

"Where I want to take you is a very special place."

"It couldn't be as special as spending time alone with you."

"I'm glad to hear that, but this is important to me. Please, princess? For me?"

"I don't have anything to wear."

"If you go upstairs to our room, you'll find that you do. It's on the bed."

"There was a delivery while I was napping?" she guessed.

"Yes."

"You really want to do this?"

"More than anything in my life."

"That sounds serious."

"It is, Lina. Very serious."

"Okay, I'll go get dressed, but you have to let me dress alone, or we won't make it out of the house."

"Already taken care of." She was right and he'd known it before she said anything, so he'd put his tux in the second bedroom—the one she'd slept in the first night—and planned to dress in there.

Lina had spent three days falling in love all over again, or admitting to herself that the love she'd felt for Sebastian when she was nineteen had never died. She had also spent those days forcing herself not to play mind games, or trick herself. She was determined not to fool herself into believing he cared about her when all he wanted was sex.

Only he *hadn't* just wanted a bedtime playmate. He'd asked her more questions like the one on the couch downstairs than she could count. He'd spent hours digging into her psyche and letting her return the favor. Just like eight years ago, only this time he had no cover story to maintain, no reason to pretend to want friendship—a *deep* friend-ship—with her.

Even so, each moment of the past three days, she'd been aware that he was actively pursuing a plan that could result in her married to another man. Or at least she'd believed that was his desire. He certainly wasn't acting like a man who expected the woman he was sharing his body with to move on to someone else.

In fact, he often made comments about the future that implied they would be spending it together.

She'd been adamant about making herself dismiss each and every one. Now she had to wonder if this time, she'd been actively fooling herself into believing that the man she loved wanted to let her go.

Oh, man…that kind of thought just led to heartache and pain. Yet Sebastian was not acting like a man who was going to hurt her. Not even sort of.

She pulled a tissue wrapping from the dress on the bed and gasped. Eight years ago, in one of their many discussions in the coffee shop on State Street, she'd mentioned to Sebastian that when she got married she wanted to wear her aunt's wedding gown. It was a white beaded, formfitting gown that would have looked in place on a 1940's starlet.

That dress was lying on their bed. Next to it was a pair of white satin heels in her size and a tiara. Not like something she'd ever worn in Marwan. Her father was a desert king and tiaras weren't de rigueur over there. But it was the kind of thing Sebastian would buy for *his* princess.

Tears burned her eyes as she wondered if she had enough courage to take one more chance with the man she was destined to love until the day she died.

In one of those sweeping moments of clarity that usually scared her half to death, she realized she didn't have the courage *not* to.

But first…she needed him to answer a question.

She found him in the room next door. He was fiddling with his bow tie, looking more nervous than she'd ever seen him.

He looked up when she walked in. "You don't like it?" he asked, his voice tight with emotion she had no trouble deciphering.

It was fear.

"I love it. You had to know I would."

He swallowed. "I hoped."

"I need you to answer a question."

"Anything for you, princess."

"I am your princess, aren't I?"

"Yes."

"That wasn't my question."

"I figured."

"Why?"

"Why what?"

"Why walk away eight years ago? Why almost walk away this time? Why the proposal? That's what this is, isn't it?" she asked, indicating the precious beaded fabric over her arm.

"That's a lot more than one question."

She didn't say anything, just waited.

His hands twisted in his tie and he yanked it off. "I'll have to use another one."

"I'll help you with it…if you answer my questions."

"Eight years ago, I believed you were under your father's legal control completely. I knew…or believed…we couldn't have a future. And frankly, that relieved me as much as it hurt."

"How come?"

"I told you about my mom."

"Yes."

"She wasn't the only woman in my life to teach me that love, affection even, is a weakness my pride cannot afford."

"Do you still believe that?"

"No."

"What happened to make you so sure of it before?"

"I've only had two other semi-serious relation-ships. The first tried to sue me for palimony after I broke it off once I'd discovered she had another man on the side. And the second dumped me for someone higher in the food chain."

"So, you thought all women were like that?"

"At least the women the men in my family are attracted to. Both my grandfather and my dad had lousy taste."

"But you don't."

His smile was brilliant and beautifully open. It made tears come to her eyes because she realized it was an entirely new expression for him. "No. I have excellent taste." A flash of pain shone in his eyes. "I only wished I'd realized that eight years ago."

"But back then you were convinced my father would and could do whatever he needed to break us apart."

"Within reason, yes. As distant as he's been with you, he is a man of honor. He won't break the law to get his way. You're no longer a citizen of his country, he can't legally order you to do—or undo—anything."

She realized Sebastian had been a lot more impacted by her father's position than she'd ever given credit. And not because he was in awe of it, but he saw it as a potential to hurt her. In his own way, her lover had been trying to save her further heartache eight years ago.

"You tried to talk to me twice."

"I couldn't let you go completely."

"I never let you go, either."

"I'm glad."

"Say it."

He grimaced.

"If you want me to wear this…you have to say it."

"Another deal?"

"Nope. This time it's pure blackmail."

He walked forward, took her into his arms and she was surprised to find he was trembling. Their eyes met.

He cupped her cheek. "I love you, my princess, today and every day throughout eternity. You are everything I ever dreamed a woman could be and more."

She wanted to tease him about being so corny, but she was too busy swallowing tears of joy. Finally she sniffled and said, "I love you, too."

"Marry me?"

"Yes."

Sebastian waited at the front of the exclusive wedding chapel for Lina's uncle to walk her down the aisle. Contacting the couple who had raised her had been a calculated risk. There was a strong chance that they would tell Lina's father of Sebastian's plans and the king and his entourage would show up to try to stop them.

But he also knew it would mean a lot to his princess to have the older couple there. So, he trusted in their love for Lina and called them.

And they'd come through. Not only had they been willing to take the private plane he had arranged for them to arrive in time, but they had brought the dress Lina now wore.

She looked like a vision…an incredible too wonderful for him but he wasn't letting her go vision. She'd pulled her long, black hair into an intricate knot on top of her head and then placed the tiara in the perfect spot. The dress accentuated her gorgeous curves and the heels lent a swing to her walk that sent his temperature straight toward the heavens.

When her uncle placed Lina's hand in Sebastian's, he felt as if his life had finally reached where it was supposed to be.

She smiled and his heart squeezed.

"Thank you," he said with fierce conviction.

The minister cleared his throat. Lina's aunt and uncle both chuckled, but she just gazed at him with a wealth of love. "For what?"

"For loving me enough not to give up."

"You're welcome. Thank you for loving me enough to come after me."

"The pleasure was entirely mine."

The rest of the ceremony was a blur of emotions and promises that rang true to the very depths of his soul.

Afterward, they had a celebratory dinner in a little known restaurant at the top floor of one of the larger downtown buildings. It was reserved for high rollers and visiting royalty. Sebastian thought his princess qualified.

His princess. For the rest of his life. Contentment poured through him in waves.

And those waves turned into a tsunami of passion when they got back to the house.

They were naked in their bed. He was poised above her, having brought her to completion once already. He throbbed with the need to be inside his wife.

He pressed until he had barely breached her most intimate flesh. "Until death."

"Until death," she repeated and lifted herself, impaling herself on him.

"I love you," he cried out as he came. "Lina, you are my life."

"Love, love, love…" she chanted over and over again as she climaxed around him, lending her pleasure to his until the circle was complete.

They were one, never to be torn asunder. He would make sure of it.

EPILOGUE

THE king of Marwan made threats and postured, but in the end, it was surprisingly easy for Sebastian and Lina to convince him to accept their marriage. It helped that she had the total support of her surrogate parents, not to mention her adopted citizenship.

The Marwanian king was not happy, but he was far from stupid. Definitely savvy enough to realize the kind of embarrassment his daughter's new allegiance could cause his country if it became public knowledge. Which it surely would if he fought against the fait accompli of Sebastian and Lina's marriage.

Her uncle had pointed it out just in case his brother-in-law was having a dense moment.

Lina had simply stated her case and then gone silent with a look Sebastian recognized as rock-hard recalcitrance. Apparently her brother recognized it, too, because he advised her father to leave be.

Sebastian ended up being good friends with the future king of Marwan, which pleased his wife so much that she experimented with some things she'd read about while studying up on human sexuality.

He made a mental note to please her often, but then that's what a man did for the woman he would love into eternity and knew with no shadow of doubt would love him just as long.

MILLS & BOON PUBLISH EIGHT LARGE PRINT TITLES A MONTH. THESE ARE THE EIGHT TITLES FOR NOVEMBER 2008.

————— ✇ —————

BOUGHT FOR REVENGE, BEDDED FOR PLEASURE
Emma Darcy

FORBIDDEN: THE BILLIONAIRE'S VIRGIN PRINCESS
Lucy Monroe

THE GREEK TYCOON'S CONVENIENT WIFE
Sharon Kendrick

THE MARCIANO LOVE-CHILD
Melanie Milburne

PARENTS IN TRAINING
Barbara McMahon

NEWLYWEDS OF CONVENIENCE
Jessica Hart

THE DESERT PRINCE'S PROPOSAL
Nicola Marsh

ADOPTED: OUTBACK BABY
Barbara Hannay

MILLS & BOON®
Pure reading pleasure™

1008 Rom LP

MILLS & BOON PUBLISH EIGHT LARGE PRINT TITLES A MONTH. THESE ARE THE EIGHT TITLES FOR DECEMBER 2008.

———————— ∅ ————————

HIRED: THE SHEIKH'S SECRETARY MISTRESS
Lucy Monroe

THE BILLIONAIRE'S BLACKMAILED BRIDE
Jacqueline Baird

THE SICILIAN'S INNOCENT MISTRESS
Carole Mortimer

THE SHEIKH'S DEFIANT BRIDE
Sandra Marton

WANTED: ROYAL WIFE AND MOTHER
Marion Lennox

THE BOSS'S UNCONVENTIONAL ASSISTANT
Jennie Adams

INHERITED: INSTANT FAMILY
Judy Christenberry

THE PRINCE'S SECRET BRIDE
Raye Morgan

MILLS & BOON
Pure reading pleasure™

1108 Rom LP